PRAISE

"*Death Aesthetic* reads like a treatise penned from the world next to this one. Rountree scours the wilds of death and finds, continually, new roads to explore, new landscapes. A moving, measured collection."
　　—Keith Rosson, author of *Fever House*

"The stories in *Death Aesthetic* craft stark poetry out of a world that is deeply unsettling even in its familiarity. Yet, in the face of man and nature's cruelty, Rountree's America preserves hope between its blood-stained teeth. This is an unforgettable collection that will settle in your marrow."
　　— J.A.W. McCarthy, Bram Stoker Award and Shirley Jackson Award finalist, author of *Sleep Alone*

"*Death Aesthetic* is textural magic. Razor-toothed prose that slits and gorgeous stitches that are pulled tight, bringing the lips of the wounds together. I say wounds because these stories hurt. Their beauty and depth and their words. My God, the words. The first tale made me gasp aloud. The second made tears flow . . . by the last one, I was wet-faced and smiling and ready to go back and do it all again. It is absolutely perfect!"
　　—John Boden, author of S*narl* and *Jedi Summer*

"Josh Rountree's stories shine a light on the human condition and its in-evitable conclusion. But death is not the villain here. It is a shapeshifter. A friend and an enemy. In Josh's deft hand, it is haunting, familiar, and endlessly fascinating."
　　—Elad Haber, author of *The World Outside*

"I've rarely had so much fun feeling such absolute grief."
　　—*FanFiAddict*

DEATH AESTHETIC

stories
by

JOSH ROUNTREE

Underland Press

Text Copyright © 2024 by Josh Rountree

Extended copyright information may be found on page 141.

This book is published by Underland Press, which is part of Firebird Creative, LLC (Clackamas, OR).

gather your most dangerous friends . . .

Edited by John Klima
Book Design and Layout by Firebird Creative

This Underland Press trade edition has an ISBN of 978-1-63023-095-1.

Underland Press
www.underlandpress.com

DEATH AESTHETIC

Dedicated to all the ghosts who haunt us.

TABLE OF CONTENTS

See That my Grave is Kept Clean — 1

The Cure for Boyhood — 9

Sounds Like Forever — 21

Their Blood Smells of Love and Terror — 40

A Red Promise in the Palm of Your Hand — 47

We Share Our Rage with the River — 59

Love Kills — 75

Constellation Burn — 79

The Green Realm — 96

Till the Greenteeth Draw Us Down — 115

Story Notes — 131

Acknowledgments — 139

"You only need enough friends to carry your casket when you're dead."

　　—Eerie Family, *After Some Deliberation They Concluded*

SEE THAT MY GRAVE IS KEPT CLEAN

Dig a hole, climb in, cover yourself in grave dirt. Not your face. You aren't ready to join the dead, not yet.

*

The bone men tend the graveyard, unaware they're being watched. You're crying because you'd lost hope of ever seeing them. They step so softly they appear to drift above the graves. Bones bright as blades in the moonlight. Tall as trees and just as slender. They clear away dead flowers and smooth out the fresh graves with white gloved hands. They straighten tombstones. They scatter leaves in artfully melancholy patterns across the steps of the stone mausoleum. On their knee bones in the muddy soil, they lean in close to the earth and whisper to the dead. This is their most important task, or so you've been told.

Someone must keep the dead company, after all.

Yellow lantern light guides your approach. The lanterns hang from posts stabbed into the earth, haphazard and crooked but always lit, no matter the hour. You suppose they have not heard of electricity in the graveyard. The night smells like thunderstorms, but so far, the rain is only a mist, and the moon still watches. Twigs snap and rocks scrape as you follow the path, but you aren't trying to hide. The bone men don't frighten you. What could you possibly have left to be afraid of? The cemetery gates are wrought iron, and they howl when you pass between them. The bone men cease their labors, turn to acknowledge your arrival. Their eye sockets are empty, but they have no trouble seeing you.

Okay, perhaps you're a *little* frightened.

But you're bold, too. Or maybe desperate. The bone men circle around; they tower like light posts, and their bones are chipped and scarred. You run your palm along one long femur and feel ice cold eternity against your skin. The bone men don't mind your touch. They are ancient things, untroubled by human concerns. When the cold begins to burn your hand, you pull it away.

You've drawn them all in close, and this is when you open your mouth and tell them why you've come. This is when you beg them for their help. And the bone men are kind, solicitous even. They can't speak but they can *communicate*, and they put you at ease. What you desire is not beyond their power, though it is certainly irregular. None among them can remember ever teaching a human to speak with the dead, but they're sure it's been done before. They have existed a very long time. They have forgotten more centuries than they remember.

They agree to help you.

And so, your lessons begin.

✱

You're not fond of the irony, but you must acknowledge it. Alicia was the one who told you about the bone men. Alicia collected stories of monsters and ghosts and trolls who lived under bridges the way some kids collect baseball cards. You'd heard her go on about the bone men a million times, but twelve-year-olds talk so much, you eventually tune them out or lose your sanity. And you were trying not to speed. Not to get caught. Trying to get home in *one piece*. Because when your mother tossed you the car keys and asked you to pick your sister up from dance class, it was either do what she asked, or confess that you'd stolen a six pack of beer from the fridge in the garage. And you hadn't even felt that drunk, not at first.

Now grief grows like lesions in your mind, and though you can't remember everything—thank God—the bits you can remember visit in high resolution. Streets slick with rain, and stoplights streaking the darkness. Alicia in her high chattering voice swearing to God that she really did see bone giants stalking the graveyard behind your house in the middle of the night, and she watched them whisper to the dead. Your head swimming and the air conditioner pumping and the rain slicing sideways. All you wanted was to rewind time and take the punishment, because you absolutely should not have been driving. Then brake lights, headlights? Screaming. An empty passenger's seat with an unfastened seatbelt hanging in limp accusation, and a yawning hole in the windshield, rimmed with blood. Like a monstrous mouth that simply swallowed your sister whole.

✱

Your lessons involve little more than the bone men placing words in your mind, and you whispering those words to the earth. Listening for a response. They caution that though you may learn to speak with the dead, you will not like what they have to say. The dead do not guard their thoughts. The dead are not *polite*. This doesn't trouble you. You'll listen to anything Alicia has to say. If only you can talk to her again, you'll gladly drown in a sea of stories about chupacabras and fairies and witches dancing beneath full moons. Let her say she hates you. Let her blame you for her death. Because you deserve it. In a way, confronting this with her might ease your burden, though that's not the end goal. You just want to tell her how sorry you are, and to hear her tiny voice again.

You haunt her tombstone like a ghoul every night, wallowing in the grave dirt, begging her to talk to you. But *Alicia Laine, Beloved Daughter and Sister, Gone Home to God*, never responds.

You can't really blame her.

The bone men counsel you to have patience. You will be able to communicate with her, *eventually*. But what is patience to creatures like these?

What have they ever lost?

✱

Nothing has ever broken you like the look in your father's eyes when he fell to his knees beside your dead sister. Nothing will ever sound so horrible as the breaking glass shriek your mother made when she spotted Alicia splayed out in the street, covered in a blanket but leaking blood into the storm drain. This version of them is awash in red and blue police lights, and drenched in rain, and it's the only version of them that remains. That moment washed your parents away and left strangers in their place, and even in your dreams, you can't remember the people who used to love you.

*

The window in your bedroom upstairs framed a view of the graveyard like a painting in a museum. You studied every play of moonlight across the yellowed grass, every naked tree branch clawing at the sky, every shadowy brush stroke on that bleak canvas. And you considered the creatures who supposedly lived there. If Alicia was to be believed, they were servants of the graveyard. They were stewards of the dead. And every night when you retreated from the heavy silence of the dinner table, when you fled to the sorry sanctuary of your bedroom, you watched out the window for them. Even though you didn't believe, you watched. Because you *needed* them to be real. You begged the universe to build such creatures into existence. And for so long, the universe ignored your desperation.

You surrounded yourself with Alicia's things. All her books on myths and monsters, every discarded doll that she'd once held dear. Unfinished homework assignments. Crayon drawings of unicorns and short stories about mermaids, written in neat block letters with a number two pencil. Hair ties and bubble gum wrappers and muddy tennis shoes. You collected all the ephemera of her life and did your best to *absorb* it. But she was still gone. There was no way to tell her you were sorry. There was no way to sit with her in the quiet gloom and listen to all the things she had to say.

Every night you studied that graveyard tableau, familiarized yourself with each graying stone bench, with every mound of fresh turned earth. And of course, with Alicia's tombstone. Some nights, you imagined a tombstone for you, right alongside hers. A matched set. And maybe that would have been better for everyone. In your darkest moods, you allowed your guilt to wander elsewhere. If your father didn't horde so much beer that he never missed a six pack, you wouldn't have been tempted. If your mother had looked at you, actually *paid attention* to anything you ever did, instead of absently tossing you the keys on her way past your bedroom door, she might have noticed you were in no shape to drive. If Alicia had just been quiet for *five seconds*, you'd have been able to focus. To push through the drunken blur, and navigate those last few blocks unscathed. But this childish escape never lasted long. Responsibility might stray, but it always found its way home to you.

Then one night, when you'd finally convinced yourself that reality could not be reshaped to fit a dead girl's imagination, you saw them. Tall and graceful and gray as storm clouds. There was not time to consider what you were seeing. You bundled up against the wet night and hurried out the back door, afraid they might disappear. Maybe they weren't really there at all. Maybe it was just your mind working overtime to torture you.

But you followed the lantern lit path, and they were waiting for you. They were *real*.

Even now, you aren't entirely sure you didn't will them into existence yourself.

✳

The bone men have instructed you well. Never, they are certain, has any human been more fluent in the language of the dead. But you still can't hear them. And though you've spoken aloud every word the bone men taught you, no one seems to be listening. Certainly not Alicia. The bone men continue their tasks while you practice; they carry on conversions with every graveyard resident like they're fast friends, and your envy boils. You ask if perhaps they can interpret for you, so you can speak with your sister that way. This suggestion is not well received. This is the only time the bone men have ever regarded you with anything but kindness. Their mood grows dark, and you understand you've broken protocol. A week passes before they will acknowledge you again, and you resign to step with more caution in the future.

After months of your nightly failure, the bone men convene to discuss among themselves what might be done to better assist you. They arrive at a consensus. It is suggested you would benefit from a closer communion with the dead. Perhaps a ritual would be beneficial. They often are in such situations. You arrive one night to find they've prepared a hole for you. A grave, next to your sister. Six feet deep, a perfect rectangle. Dirt piled up beside it. You have no desire to enter that hole, but the bone men assure you everything will be fine. This is certain to bring you closer to your sister. You hesitate. The bone men sense your unease, but they don't fully understand it.

What could be more comfortable and welcoming than a freshly dug grave?

One of them lifts you in his arms and places you gently into the earth, like a newborn child into a crib. The bone men look over the edge of the grave like proud parents, unable to hide the fondness they feel. You writhe in the wet darkness. There is no comfort to be found amid the tangle of underground roots and jagged rocks. But comfort is not the goal. They reassure you as their hands begin shoveling dirt over the top of your body. Not to worry, they won't cover your face. Living in this world is hard, but they understand life is not a burden you are quite prepared to divest. Not yet. This will bring you close, though. Close enough to communicate, almost assuredly.

When they've finished, only your face remains uncovered. No moving your arms, no kicking out. Never did you expect the soil to sit so heavy on top of you. Panic flaps about in your chest like too many birds in a tiny cage. The bone men are delighted, and they still watch you from above, blanking out the stars and the lantern light, leaving nothing but black shadows across your resting place. Part of you wants to scream, but the soil is pressed so tight around your chin and cheeks that you can only whimper. The ground is cold. The air is wet and thin. And if it were not for the gentle soothing of the bone men, you'd never be able to settle down long enough to just listen. They pluck out the anxiety from your chest and replace it with resolve. They promise not to abandon you in your grave. You breathe deep. And you hear whispers, a rush of white noise, traveling through the hard packed earth.

The dead are talking to you.

Or rather, the dead are talking amongst themselves, and you're eavesdropping on their conversations.

Having learned their language, you understand what's being said. But the words come in such a rush, it's hard to isolate any one speaker. You mouth a few sentences, trying to get a word in, but the dead won't slow down for the living, and their chatter proceeds at a lightning pace. They worry about nothing and keep no secrets. They don't yearn for life or pine for the living. There's no concern about what came before, and some of them don't seem to remember living at all. You try to speak, again and again. You mumble Alicia's name and struggle to pick her voice out of the din, but it's all so overwhelming. You imagine her cold body, buried just a few feet from yours. Why is it so hard to connect? You wonder if, perhaps, she's already forgotten you entirely.

The bone men look down at you with pity.

Eventually they dig you up, set you on your feet.

They promise Alicia will talk to you someday, but you don't hold out much hope.

*

The strangers who used to be your parents catch you sneaking in from your night in the graveyard, and they aren't happy. Your mother's voice is sharp as a sword and your father wields guilt like a truncheon. You stand muddy and wild-eyed in the kitchen as they remind you that *you're the only thing they have left in the world*. They've hardly spoken to you in months, and they've forgotten that you're someone they used to love. So, when you begin to argue, they let slip every accusation they've been holding inside. They remind you that *this whole thing is your fault*. They aren't monsters. They're just broken. But you wish they'd go back to being strangers. Better than revealing the people they've become.

*

Having spent time in the grave, your bed feels too soft. The mattress sinks in the middle, and you long for hard packed clay. Eventually you give up on sleep, stare out the window, and watch the bone men tend to their charges. Every tombstone straightened. Every grave swept clean of debris. There's something beautiful and sad about the devotion they show to the dead. Tears well in your eyes when you consider that Alicia will never be alone.

The bone men will always be there for her.

Downstairs, your parents argue deep into the night. They poison one another with blame. Nothing beautiful remains for them in this world. They're dead and rotting and don't even know it yet. Maybe all of you are. Holding on to a life that has nothing left to offer. You consider going downstairs, entering the fray. Maybe you can figure out some way to reassemble what's been broken. But nothing will bring Alicia back, and *this whole thing is your fault*. Instead, you stand at your window with your palms pressed against the cold glass, remembering the smell of wet earth and the taste of it in your mouth. You remember earthworms, burrowing in close, and your sister, cold company in the ground next to you. You watch the bone men, and consider the ease with which they connect. Like the language of the dead is carved into their bones.

And finally, you understand.

The bone men can't speak with the dead because they have some gift that you don't.

It's because they've lost something you still have.

*

You've made a decision that pleases the bone men.

They'd have suggested this course of action straight away, but people tend to value their lives more than their deaths. It's a notion foreign to them, but one they've come to accept over the centuries. The bone men know the truth of things. They *understand*. Life is quick and loud, like snapping your fingers. Death is beautiful and serene. Death is a slow boat down a peaceful river. Existence is eternal. The bone men don't understand why anyone would value a fleeting moment of sharp, bright pain over the endless repose of death.

Your grave beckons. The bone men hold your hand, help you down into the hole, all the while reassuring you that now *everything will be okay*. You're so grateful for their gentle ministrations. This time you're ready. The bone men cover you entirely. Fill the grave. Erect a tombstone. Leave orchids in a brass vase.

They swaddle you in the earth.

Your lungs grow still, and there's nothing to distract you anymore. The dead invite you into the conversation.

Alicia is there. Alicia speaks.

This whole thing is your fault.

And, of course, she's right.

But at least you have forever to make amends.

THE CURE FOR BOYHOOD

The boy used to be a coyote until his parents decided to cure him.

✳

This is how that happens. The coyote is caught unawares climbing back through his bedroom window, still reeling from the darkness. Fur falls away as his body contorts and the teenaged boy inside unwillingly shrugs off his animal skin in long strips, like orange rind being peeled away with a paring knife. It's in this bloody, in-between state of existence that the parents grab hold of their child and press him onto the bed. There's much wrestling with ropes and the boy is still a bit stronger than he'll be when his human self emerges entirely, but the parents are well prepared and binding their little animal to the bed is necessary and good.

The parents have seen all the movies and rejected more extreme solutions. Silver bullets, for one. And fire, another well-known method for destroying monsters. But this isn't really a monster—this is their only son.

Wolfsbane then? Not exactly, but close enough.

There's a woman who lives on the north side of the railroad tracks. Children call her witch, hag, bruja. They dare one another to knock on her door. Every child knows someone who knows someone who went inside that house, never to be seen again, and the mythology of childhood is unshakable. The woman's house leans in such a way that the next strong western wind might blow it over, and the north side of the tracks is the *bad* side of the tracks, so it was sheer desperation that drove the boy's parents to knock on that door.

That's how much they think they love him.

The father struggles to hold his son in place. Coyote blood still thrums behind the boy's eyeballs. He releases a howl that freezes his mother in her approach. She holds a small fabric bag, no larger than her palm, a thing of supposed magic from the woman across the tracks. Filled with grave dirt, snake teeth, mesquite thorns. Impossible to say what else. And she knows what must be done, but she loses her nerve for the span of that howl, captured by her fear of the animal she still can't believe she gave birth to. Then her husband shouts, and she moves. She's still thinking of those movies, believing that if she's bitten it might be *her* next time, tied up on the bed, so she is careful, so careful, to avoid her son's teeth when she shoves the bag into his mouth.

The father grabs the boy's chin, forcing him to bite down. Teeth and thorns and blood. But there's already so much blood.

Whatever is in the bag squirms to life, lodges itself in the boy's throat so tight he can't even cough. He tries to howl his parents into submission again but there's no room left for noise anymore.

The boy goes still.

And when he wakes, he's cured.

✳

Removing the boy's animal nature doesn't cleanse him of all the things his parents hate, but for the most part, their minds are at ease, content in the knowledge of what he is *not* doing. Prowling. Peering at sleeping victims through unlocked windows. Robbing henhouses. They imagine so many things. The boy would think it was hilarious if his parents' fears hadn't stolen the best part of him. Even werewolves, which he most certainly is not, must have better things to do.

The truth of it is, the boy just likes to run.

Half of the town he lives in dried up and blew away before he was born. Acres of cotton fields surround the town on all sides, the only barrier against the thirsty West Texas horizon. On all fours, the boy speeds between the rows, throwing up clouds of dust behind him. There is nothing to stop him from running forever, save for the sunlight that will always force him back into the boy-shaped thing that he does not entirely understand. He's afraid of what might happen if the sun catches him outside, if he transforms back into a naked, gangly creature there on some farmer's land. So, he's always careful to get home before sunrise.

This used to be a boom town. A place with an air-conditioned movie theater and a record store that Elvis Presley visited in the fifties. A Woolworth's five and dime *and* a Montgomery Wards. The buildings remain, but what they were can only be glimpsed through the ragged reality of today. The town and its people are bone tired, yet they lay awake, wide-eyed, and never do anything about it.

A somber oil refinery chugs along at the edge of town, burning off chemicals into the night skies, flames blinking like fireflies in the distance. A monument to yesterday's prosperity.

Bits and pieces remain of the airbase built in the forties. Bomber crews trained here during the war, and fighter pilots after that. The boy's parents remember flyboys revving their Corvettes and Chargers through the bustle of downtown. Date nights at the country club. Fancy dinners at the steakhouse out on the highway. Then the airbase closed, and anyone who remained that didn't *have* to be here moved far away.

That's when the slow death began.

That's when the town changed from a place that is, to a place that used to be.

But that airbase? The bones of it are still here.

This is where the boy really loves to run. Buckled and bearded with weeds, the runways remain. An air traffic control tower commandeered by snakes and daddy long legs keeps watch as he speeds through the darkness. He is fast, so fast that sometimes he thinks he might lift off from the earth like the B-17s and P-51s and T-6 Texans that he'd assembled piece by piece from Revell model kits when he was younger. He could smell the chemical punch of the model glue as surely as the diesel exhaust from the planes as they lifted off, tearing away from him so fast in his mind that he could never keep up. The boy is winded, rolls to a stop in the tall grass at the edge of the runway and laughs.

All of this is gone now too.

Like the town, the boy isn't what he used to be.

✱

The boy sits squashed between his mother and father at church. The threadbare cushion that runs the length of the pew seems designed for maximum discomfort. He wriggles his way into a less miserable position and his mother clamps one birdlike hand on his knee. Runways and cotton fields call to him. The world moves. But in here it feels like he's holding his breath. Like the simple act of taking air in and out of his lungs is far too riotous. A sin beyond the pale.

The preacher is a kind enough man, always nice to the boy, a boisterous fellow who enjoys kicking back at the church picnics with a six pack and a carton of unfiltered cigarettes. Someone the parishioners appreciate because he embraces the same petty sins they do. But his sermon moves with all the speed of honey pouring from a plastic bottle and even the most devout are sneaking looks at their wristwatches. Standing in front of everyone, both hands gripping the podium and draped in his long black robe, the preacher is not the same man you might encounter on Saturdays in the café, sipping black coffee. He has donned the trappings of godliness. As a young man he chose this disguise for himself, and even though it may no longer fit him perfectly, when he puts it on, the preacher can pretend he too is beyond these simple sins.

Disguises are handy things.

Despite the fact they are only weeks removed from stealing their son's soul, the mother and father sit with their backs straight as yardsticks, comfortable in their pride. They'd surely considered asking the droning preacher to help with their problem, but if their son was really possessed by some sort of demon as they suspected, was that really the domain of a Protestant religion? Exorcists fell in the Catholic camp, and there were no Catholics here, at least not on the *good* side of the tracks. And besides, there were some problems the church could solve and others that were best taken care of at home.

Kept secret.

Once the boy would have been able to hear heartbeats slowing down as the preacher's drawl hardened around them, sealing everyone in place like ancient insects in amber. He would have smelled the sweat beading on the brows of everyone in the choir loft and the bacon grease stench of everyone's fried breakfast.

But the world has dulled around him. Now a thing to be endured rather than experienced.

The cure his parents gave him is lodged tight in the boy's throat like a bit of food he can't swallow. Speaking requires a certain effort. His body rebels, but the cure remains intact.

The boy lets his tongue slide across twin canines, still sharp. His fingers tap a rhythm against his thighs. Mother's clawed hand tightens.

When the air conditioner kicks on with a sound like a tractor engine turning over, it drowns out the preacher's voice. The air conditioner doesn't make a dent in the heat. The sanctuary is an oven, and the boy imagines the massive organ pipes behind the choir are smokestacks, choking out the earthly remains of the whole captured congregation. They've been laid low with apathy by this endurance test of a sermon and are content to simply burn to death in this charnel house without further resistance.

It's all too much.

The boy sloughs off his mother's hand and stands, accidentally knocking her hymnal to the floor. The preacher stops speaking mid-sentence. He stares at the boy with his mouth slightly ajar as if he's expecting a question and readying an answer.

The boy pushes past his father, into the aisle, and escapes. It's hotter outside, but here he can feel the wind against him.

Here he can take a breath.

✳

Fields of cattle, cotton farms, land razed flat to support oil derricks in their lonely, ceaseless labors. All separated from the unspooling highway by barb wire strung between mesquite posts, taut and toothy. The boy has biked here, miles out of town, and though the bike is no substitute for the speed of his own four feet, it's all he has now.

Coyote carcasses hang from the fence posts in bunches, some of them desiccated to the point their pelts are nearly transparent, others still black with blood. This is how farmers endeavor to keep other coyotes off their land. Away from their livestock. As if their dead brothers are warning enough to stave off the hunger that draws them close to Man's reach in the first place.

The boy steps down on one strand of barb wire, pressing it to the ground, while he lifts another up, careful not to grab the barbs. He widens the gap between the two strands enough to fit, barely snagging the back of his tee shirt as he heads his way through, a maneuver that every child in this place has mastered before they are in middle school.

And he is standing deep in the turned earth, eyes set on the far end of the field where all the cotton rows seem to converge like an arrowhead at the same magical point. He knows it's an optical illusion, but it's a place he desperately wants to be.

So, the boy runs.

He's careful not to step on the low, leafy cotton plants, crisp and dry and thirsty for the sort of rain they haven't seen this season. The thinnest sliver of white shows itself in the shadows of their growth. When the season draws to a close, the brown bolls will split open to reveal the cotton fibers within. The field will look like two feet of late summer snow.

At the far edge of the field, a rusted green tractor clatters along, plowing between the rows. Men with wide brimmed hats bend their backs to hoes, chopping at the desperate slivers of grassbur and thistle that shoot up beneath the plants, too close for the plow to catch.

There is only so much sustenance in the earth. Only so much food for hungry animals. Only so many paying jobs to be had under the weight of a blistering sun.

Everything in this place is consumed with its own struggle for life.

The boy remembers how light his feet were when he would race these rows at night, a shape built to cut the darkness. But the sun is high and he's just a boy. His progress is sluggish. His too-large feet sink deep into the loose soil.

His lungs burn like brushfires.

He's not going anywhere.

Eventually the boy tires himself out, no closer to his destination than when he started running. He lies on the ground, eyes closed, the sun burning red against the backs of his eyelids.

Flies drink the sweat from his brow, but he doesn't bother to swat them away.

✱

There was a time the boy would slip out through his window every night, assume his true shape, and *live*. Always finding his way home before his parents came in to wake him for school. Always half asleep in class, daydreaming about empty streets and stars spilled across a cloudless sky. The air was juniper and creosote and the tickle of sand in his nose.

The boy can still taste those nights in his teeth.

Now he sneaks out that same window and mounts his bike. Pedals under the streetlights, trying to find something of himself again. His instincts have been caged, but not killed, he thinks. The boy can feel the coyote blood still inside, and when he pedals harder, his bones shift against the underside of his skin, eager to snap and bend and reform.

His progress is aimless, he has nowhere to be.

So, like others his age, he winds up at the drive-in.

The great beacon that pulls them all in is a tall neon sign in the shape of a wagon wheel. Cars idle at the food order stations, engines still running so the air conditioning doesn't shut off. The place exists in its own illuminated bubble, and just beyond the reach of that light is where the boy climbs off his bike and watches, no more eager to leave the safety of darkness than when he was a coyote.

Preternatural senses aren't necessary to breathe in the night and understand this place entirely. Onion rings and corndogs. Burgers charred black and milkshakes so thick you have to let them melt before you can suck them through the straw. And everywhere, the hot smell of summer sand blown in from the farms. Collected on windowsills, on plastic tabletops, on dashboards littered with greasy food wrappers and dead wasps.

The boy counts the faces he used to know in elementary school. Eight or ten he remembers well, though in a town this size, he recognizes nearly everyone.

A few kids in denim jackets and black concert tees crowd around one of the walk-up tables. A guitar solo erupts from the jam box they've stationed amid a scattering of French fry bags and ketchup packets.

A couple of pickup trucks are parked, waiting for food. The cabs are tall enough that the guys inside don't have to remove their cowboy hats. They sneak drinks from longnecks, then shove the bottles back between their legs.

Teenagers yell from car to car, and a girl shrieks with laughter. It's an unsettling sound, like sheet metal being torn in half.

This is summer, deep in the night.

Nobody is thinking about tomorrow.

The boy is slick with sweat, and everyone else is too. Even so, the heavy metal kids at the walk-up table don't shuck their jackets. That would be like removing a layer of skin.

And none of the cowboys roll up their long sleeves. They wear the outfit inherited from their parents and their grandparents. Jeans and boots and shirtsleeves buttoned at the wrist to protect against the sun and snakes and the thousand other perils that their ancestors faced.

They bear the heat and don't complain.

The boy doesn't fault them.

He understands it's worth a little suffering to be the person you want to be.

They were all the same once, when they were younger. Before they diverged and transformed into the creatures they are now. Most of them have become exactly who they want to be.

Or, at least, who they want to be *right now*.

The boy dumps his bike and walks into the light.

He finds an empty table at the heart of the chaos. Girls, their bangs blown high with cheap hairspray, pass with trays full of food. Boys follow, bathed in grocery store cologne.

One arm, sliding around a slender waist.

Every one of them, believing they've achieved their final shapes.

Once perfected, nothing will ever warp them.

The boy's bones shudder so violently that he nearly falls off the metal bench that's bolted to the ground beside the table. He clings to the table with both hands, fighting to still himself.

A pickup truck brakes into a space nearby, headlights hitting the tables dead on. A pair of cowboys climb out, loud and laughing and fresh off a couple hours of two-stepping at the dancehall out on the highway. A year older than the boy is, then. Just old enough to get into bars with an underage *X* drawn on the back of the hand with magic marker.

The boy is wondering why he came out of hiding when the cowboys get so close that he can smell the menthol smoke from the middle-aged divorcées they've been dancing with.

Did he think somebody here would help him?

He convulses so hard that he finally draws the wrong kind of attention. A couple of cigarette butts come flying his way. Someone tosses a half empty beer can that skids across the tabletop and fizzes out in the grass. One of the cowboys puts a hand on the boy's shoulder, comes close enough to speak right in his ear and the music is so loud now that the boy can't make out what the guy is saying.

He's too *close*.

The boy opens his mouth to tell the guy to back off, but that choking ball of magic is still lodged tight in his throat and he can only produce an animal hiss.

The guy keeps talking. Might be telling the boy it's best he hit the road. Might be asking if he needs an ambulance.

It doesn't matter anymore.

The boy's bones clench up like a fist.

He turns, grabs the cowboy by the back of the head, pulls him close. Opens his mouth wide and tears into the guy's throat.

Canines longer than they should be, rending.

The cowboy's Stetson hits the ground, catches a burst of wind, and skips away across the parking lot. His hands grasp at the remains of his throat, fingers flexing like he's working to reassemble himself.

There is so much blood.

The boy feels it hot on his face, and in that instant the world around him stops like a watch that hasn't been wound.

Then the cowboy drops to his knees, and everyone exhales. They're digging in their gloveboxes for revolvers. Retrieving tire irons and baseball bats from truck beds. Yelling for the carhop to call the cops.

The boy flees the light, finds his bike in the brush, and bolts. Ignoring the screaming, the angry shouts.

He's really moving now.

✱

Seventeen and no license to drive because he never needed one. Wheels would only slow a coyote down. But the boy on the bicycle wishes for more speed as the glow of the drive-in disappears behind him like a candle being snuffed out.

He wants to go home, but there's no *home* left now.

He can taste the dead man in his mouth.

Bike tires rattle over the train tracks as he pedals for the only place he can think of to go. That thing in his throat is practically pulling him there. There's only one place that people like his parents could have gone searching for a cure around here. The boy's not stupid. He's heard all the stories.

He's looking for the house that leans.

When he finds the right street, it's potted and buckled, and there's only an empty pole where a street sign used to hang. The boy rides to the end, where the asphalt gives way to a field of tall grass and clawing weeds. The wind chases him toward it, and he imagines that every discarded thing in town must eventually find its way here. Empty Coke bottles, rusted wheel rims, cigarette butts, all drawn to this place, helpless to resist its pull.

One streetlight stands tall, its light yellow and flickering.

Somewhere in the grass, animals move, though the boy cannot identify them. They are drawn here too, to the very edge of civilization. The outskirts of town.

The space just beyond the light.

There are people not so far away who don't know this part of their town exists. And they would certainly never come here if they did.

The boy has never been here before, but he's pretty sure his parents have.

He abandons his bike at the sidewalk and steps into the yard of the leaning house. But this is not the haunted house from the stories. Windows remain unbroken. Screams don't emanate from within. The grass beneath his sneakers has been mowed recently enough that the boy can smell the clippings. And the house stands firm. It might lean just a bit on its foundation, but why wouldn't it after a half a century of life? The house is tired, perhaps, but so are the rest of the houses on this street. The rest of the houses in this town too, if we're being honest.

The boy wasn't sure what to expect when he came here, but it certainly wasn't just more of the same.

He climbs the porch steps and the thing in his throat begins to thrash. His bones feel like they're lengthening, but the skin around them makes no accommodation.

His fists hammer at the screen door.

The witch peers out through the slit in her curtains but has no intention of answering. Her work is already finished. Even as the boy's face lurches in pain, she can see the resemblance he bears to his father. The man who begged her to cure his son. She gave that man what he asked for, if not exactly what he wanted. She has lived a very long time and understands that life will unfold as it wants to, no matter how desperately one might want to nudge it one way or another. Hers is not to buck the will of creation. Hers is only to serve its purpose.

Outside on the porch she sees her old pair of gardening gloves, a potted cactus, a couple of lawn chairs, a wrought iron table with a half glass of water left behind. A boy on his knees. He wishes he could push enough air from his lungs to scream. The thing in his throat catches fire and threatens to burn him down from the inside. He whispers prayers. He begs someone to open the door and help him. Grabs his own throat, squeezes, tries to choke up whatever is inside him.

Both of his hands find the table, working to steady himself, his whole body shaking. And right there in front of him sits that glass of water. Condensation on the glass. Somehow still cold.

Like someone poured it and left it just for him.

The boy grabs the cup and drinks it down.

Howls fill the night. Animals lifting their voices in the tall grass. The boy wails in answer. For a second, he thinks maybe he finally managed to choke up the thing in his throat, then he feels it going to work in his stomach. Settling deep inside him, warm and alive.

Hungry to remake him.

The porch light comes on at the house across the street. Someone shouts from next door. The neighborhood wakes, sleepy eyes trying to get a look at whoever is making so much racket at the strange old lady's house. The boy crouches on her porch, someone else's blood drying into the folds of his tee shirt, trying to stand, trying to hide. Failing at both.

So, he does what comes naturally. He scampers down the steps on all fours. He can hear the thunderclap of bones breaking beneath his skin, but he doesn't feel the pain. Just the slow inferno rising inside to burn away all the parts of himself that he doesn't need anymore. He kicks his shoes off, feels the sidewalk against his toes and his palms. Muscles bind, twist, lengthen, propel him toward the tall, swaying grass.

The animal inside is really moving now.

In the field he races through the dense weeds. Every thorn and every knife-like blade of grass peel away a little bit more of the boy until he's left everything behind. Blood and meat and ripped denim. Toenails and flat, stubby teeth. Preachers and parents and kindly old witches.

Then the coyote breaks out, beyond the grass, and there is nothing ahead of him but land, flat and endless.

He might run forever.

The coyote used to be a boy. But now he's cured.

SOUNDS LIKE FOREVER

We hiked into the woods, trying to find the place where you died. Gray clouds sank from the heavens, chewed away the tops of the pine trees and spat drizzle down on our heads. Thunder rumbled in the distance, but apart from that, the forest was quiet, like everything that had once lived there joined you in the afterlife. It was midday, but the forest absorbed every sliver of sun that made it through the clouds. I whispered a song lyric you wrote, the one about how *death can't live in the light*, and I think I finally understood what you were trying to say.

Marcus's older brother was a sheriff's deputy, and he told us where to find the crash site. Marcus led the way, April a step behind him, one hand always clutching his flannel shirttail. I trailed after them in my yellow slicker and chunky boots. Marcus and April were laughing about something, but I was in no mood. You'd been dead a month, and I felt like I'd been crying ever since. For them, this was a lark, a chance to collect a salacious story to share with the other kids on Monday. But I needed to see where it happened. I needed to recapture something I'd lost.

Marcus and April, they listened to your music. I mean, pretty much everyone did, right?

But I don't think they ever really *heard* it.

"Oh shit, Jen. Look at this."

April waved me closer, and when I caught up, I thought we'd stumbled across an old logging road that had been reclaimed by undergrowth. But then I realized what I was seeing. This was the trail the plane had cut through the trees. It looked like someone had taken a giant pencil eraser and wiped a straight line through the forest for a few hundred feet. The treetops were splintered, sheared off by the wings. We followed the path of the crash, like children in a fairy tale, afraid of what we might find at the end, but unable to turn back.

As we walked, my mind traced the last seconds of your life. I hoped you were sleeping when the plane went down. But if not, if you were belted in tight to the Cessna's window seat as the plane engine trailed smoke and the treetops began to claw at the belly of the fuselage, I hoped there were angels waiting there to carry you away. Before the wings snapped off. Before the jet fuel inferno.

I don't believe in God, but I could still hope.

"Oh man, this is so fucking cool!" Marcus sprinted the last bit to the clearing, dragging April behind him.

The place where the plane had come to rest, the place where they'd found the *wreckage*, was a fire-blackened bowl carved into the world. All the trees at the periphery were charred blades stabbing at the sky. The drizzle had grown into a steady rain, and the ground was gray sludge. Nothing remained of the plane, of course. The FBI, or FAA, or whoever had already combed this place to remove all the remains, to remove the *evidence*, and I'd seen enough movies to know they'd probably reconstructed the plane in some warehouse, assembled it piece by piece like a dinosaur skeleton, trying to figure out what had killed it.

Not that it mattered to me. Nothing would change the fact you were dead.

"It happened right here," said April.

"Wow, you're a fucking genius," said Marcus.

They'd been holding hands, and April let go. "You don't have to always be an asshole."

"I kind of do," he said. "It's my thing."

Marcus put an arm around April and pulled her into a rough hug that I could tell she didn't want. I wished Marcus had stayed home. April was a different person when he wasn't around, but she was drawn to him for reasons I couldn't understand. He was cute, sure. But the artfully messy hair and broken grin weren't disguise enough to hide the trouble lurking inside him. I wanted to tear off that mask and show April who Marcus really was, but I suspected she already knew.

They sniped back and forth, sharp voices echoing back off the cloud cover.

I sat down on the ground, ran my fingers through the grime, wondering if this wet ash belonged to you. Everything in the clearing was burned except for an unlikely scattering of dark-bladed plants that grew in quiet defiance. A sign, maybe, that the forest had already forgotten your death, was starting to breathe again. The air was heavy, and the earth drew me close until I had my cheek pressed against the ground, and I swear I could hear your heart beating against me. No part of you remained there, not really, but I wanted so much to have you back in the world.

April noticed me on the ground, knelt, and put a hand on my shoulder. "Hey, are you okay? Let me help you sit up. You're getting soot and stuff all over you. It's kind of gross."

"Holy shit, look at this!" said Marcus.

I sat up and tried wiping the muck off my hands and onto my slicker, but I mostly just smeared it around. Marcus knelt beside us, not to offer any help, but to get a closer look at the weird plants that fanned out from the place where you died.

"It's pot," he said. "Just growing here in the wild. Probably get you super fucked up, right?"

I fanned my palms over the tiny plants, saw the rainwater beading on their surfaces. They were shaped like marijuana leaves but weren't the right color; these were a swarm of black and purple, limned in yellow. They reminded me of fresh bruises. Marcus picked a few handfuls, shoved them in his pockets, chattering about how he was going to make a mint selling all that shit to asshole freshmen. I know you weren't buried there. You were somewhere else now. But it felt to me like he was stealing flowers off your grave.

On our way back out of the forest, though, I started to wonder. Did you leave those plants for us to find?

All these years later, I still don't know.

✱

April came to my house a few days after our trek into the woods, dug a joint out of her purse, and told me to smoke it.

"Not interested," I said.

"Jen, for real, you need to try this."

She held the joint out to me, revealing a trail of yellow bruises on her forearm; another one, dark and purple wrapped her wrist like a bracelet. I took it from her in a hurry so she'd lower her arm, so she could pull her jacket sleeve down and neither of us would have to acknowledge what I'd seen. She sat down on the beanbag by my bedroom window, a kind of smirk on her face, like she was daring me to start in on her again.

"Not in the mood," I said. "I'll save it for later."

"As long as you promise me you'll smoke it."

"Why are you so concerned with getting me high? If I want pot, I know where to find it."

"It's not pot," she said. "It's graveweed."

"Say what?"

April grinned, her eyes half closed but shining with glee, feeling no pain.

"It's the stuff Marcus dug up at the crash site," she said. "He started calling it that, and the name stuck."

Gray rain slapped the window behind April. It was late afternoon but already my bedroom was so dark that shadows webbed the distance between us. The cloud cover turned my bedroom into a sort of cave, a place where I felt safe, because, of course, I've always been more comfortable in gloomy places. Like you sang, *the things I'm afraid of don't hide in the dark.* Yeah, that one hit me square in the chest. Still does. And usually, having my best friend lounging there with me, with the candles bleeding light up the walls and the rain battering at the roof, that would be just like heaven. Like *right then, right there,* everything was perfect.

Except that day, April felt *off.*

Less like a friend and more like an intruder in my private space.

"The name stuck?" I said. "What are you saying, he gave it a stupid name and he's selling it?"

"Forty bucks a baggie," said April. "This weed isn't normal. Marcus already had to go back and get more."

"He went out there without me? I thought he was joking about selling that stuff. What an asshole."

"Wait, are you pissed?" she asked.

"Yeah, I'm pissed!" I said. "That's like sacred ground now. Marcus shouldn't be going back there to dig the place up."

"First, he's not *digging the place up,*" said April. "He's just picking some plants, okay? Second, you don't own the fucking *death site,* Jen. Get over this mood you're in. I know you're way into music, but it's not like a friend of yours died."

"It's not that easy," I said. "I thought you understood there was more to this than that."

"I do," she said.

"Then what, you don't care?"

April stared at me with her mouth slightly ajar, like she was trying out words to make sure whatever she said next didn't break something between us that couldn't be fixed.

She looked so perfect with her blonde hair streaked with pink, and the flannel shirt and denim jacket she wore to be stylish instead of to *keep the fucking rain off her back*, and I drew my hooded sweatshirt tighter around me, crossed my arms like I was trying to hide whatever it was she saw in me, but that's okay, because it was never about her being *her* and me being . . . whoever I am, because she was the one friend who understood me.

April was the only one I ever told about the night my mom and I escaped Lubbock in the middle of the night, left in just our pajamas and flip flops, and headed north in her old Bronco that smoked like a campfire. All I grabbed on the way out the door was my portable CD player and my copy of *Sounds Like Forever.* My hair was wet with blood and the headphones became sticky, but your music, your *words,* helped me push back against the memory of my dad putting my head through the glass coffee table.

Doing worse things maybe to Mom.

This was three years before you died, so I was fourteen.

Which is to say, April *knew.* She knew your record pretty much saved my life. And she knew what it was to need to escape someone, no matter if she was willing to admit it to herself yet or not.

"Of course, I care," she said. "I'm sorry. Can we turn down the heat a little? I just came to hang out. I didn't mean to pick a fight. Are we okay?"

"We're okay," I said.

"Jen, are you crying?" she asked. "For real, I'm sorry."

I hadn't realized I was crying, so I wiped away the tears with my sleeve. "I'm not mad. We're cool. I was just thinking about when we first got to Washington, Mom convinced herself we'd just be at my grandparents' house long enough for Dad to cool off. We just sat around their kitchen table for a week, Mom chain-smoking Virginia Slims, telling me not to worry, everything was going to work out. Even with one eye still swollen shut, she kept trying to convince me Dad wasn't really a bad person. Just fooling herself, trying to hang on to a hope that had died before I was even born. And I'll tell you a secret. I didn't really care. I knew he'd be glad we were gone. And I knew if she did go back, I wasn't going with her."

"Well, I'm glad you stayed," said April.

"Me too." I tossed the joint she'd given me onto my bedside table. "So, what do you mean, this isn't normal pot?"

"Told you, it's not pot," she said. "It's graveweed."

"Yeah, graveweed. Fine. Whatever."

"It gets you stoned," she said. "But not like normal stoned. You, of all people, are gonna love it."

"Why *me of all people*?" I asked.

"I kind of don't want to say much until you try it, because I think you'll just roll your eyes at me and toss it in the trash. Just let me know what you think?"

"I will. When I'm feeling in the mood."

"No, tonight. So we can talk about it tomorrow."

"If it will shut you up."

April smiled. "It will."

I hadn't wanted to spend my night stoned on what was likely skunk weed that would burn my lungs and make my head spin, but I wanted even less to argue about it with my best friend when there were more important things to worry about. April stayed for another hour, and we talked about anything but graveweed and her dangerous choice in boyfriends, but when I eventually walked her to the front door, I couldn't help but prod at that sore spot one more time.

"Anytime you need to talk, I'm here," I said. "Some people are just not worth it. It's hard to figure that out sometimes."

"Let's not start fighting again." April stood in the doorway with her car keys in her hands, not mad, but eager to be anywhere else. My mom's boyfriend, Hobie, watched the tension rise from his spot on the living room couch. Hobie was surly, always half drunk, and had a habit of looking at me in a way forty-something dudes shouldn't look at teenaged girls. Mom came in from the kitchen where she was frying something for dinner, put a beer in his hand and kissed his head, but he never stopped watching us.

"I'm not fighting," I said. "I just think you need to be careful."

"I don't need a sermon," April said. "I just need you to trust me, okay?"

"Okay, just . . . drive safe, I guess."

April nodded, jogged out to her car, through the drizzle. Not for the first time, I thought about how out of place she was in all this north-western gloom. Even her name sounded like sunshine.

I stood there in the open doorway for a long time, breathing in the rain, not wanting to go back inside with the smell of hot grease and ashtrays. I mouthed a few of your song lyrics, smiled when I tripped across *forever lives someplace else now*, because I remembered listening to that one over and over during our escape from Texas. I didn't under-stand then what you meant by those words, but I didn't care, because on that long drive, on the run from my fucked-up life with no clue what was ahead, I understood what it meant to *me*.

After a time, Hobie hollered at me to close the door before I let all the fucking rain in, so I did.

Then I stalked past him on the way to my bedroom, wondering how any of us managed to survive in a world so full of predators.

✳

I smoked the graveweed joint while sitting on my bed, schoolbooks scattered about, and one of your songs playing low from the CD player on my nightstand. Your voice whispered to me about *dead angel rain* and *children who break like glass*, and I absorbed it all, certain your songs had a supernatural hold on my life. All teenagers probably feel that way about their music, but I don't know.

You were *my* rock star. You were my voice.

I felt like I didn't know what to say without you.

Pot usually made me happy, but this shit was seriously depressing, so I took the last drag and tossed the roach into an empty soda can. I waved the smoke out the open window and lit a candle to scent the room with vanilla. I lay back on the bedspread, watched the candlelight play over the posters that covered my walls. Nine Inch Nails. Stone Temple Pilots. Nirvana and Mother Love Bone and Soundgarden. And on the ceiling over my bed, a nearly life-sized poster of you on stage, screaming at the world with only a guitar to shield you from all its horrors.

God, I loved you so fucking much.

After a time, the room started to go fuzzy around the edges, and I noticed a corner of your poster peel away from the ceiling. It kept going, like someone was rolling it up to put it back in the tube, and I saw then that the poster had been hiding a massive hole that leaked light down on my bed like honey, golden and sticky.

"Oh."

Your dead tattooed fingers wriggled around the edges of the hole, clawing to escape, and I listened as voices—not just a few, but hundreds, thousands, maybe every voice that ever was—sang out *find me cold in death, find you on the ground, broken in tears* and your words weren't just coming from my stereo anymore, they were coming from *everywhere*. And when your face appeared, when you crawled down from that hole in the ceiling and stood at the foot of my bed with that light oozing down across your shoulders, tears flooded my eyes and a scream lodged in my throat.

Your eyes locked with mine, and I'm pretty sure I stopped breathing altogether.

The voices kept singing your words, and you joined them. *I'm gone, long gone, but you'll find me.*

I've heard those lyrics a million times.

How could I have ever thought I'd lost you for good?

All these years later, I think maybe your songs were predictive. You knew what was going to happen to me, what would happen to you, before it ever did. Or maybe my brain was making connections that weren't there, like that phenomenon, pareidolia, where the human brain wants to make sense of things, so it finds familiar faces in clouds or the image of a barking terrier in a pinewood knot.

You didn't come any closer, but you stood *right there* for so long. Breathing and singing and wearing that same Scratch Acid tee shirt that you wore on the cover of *Rolling Stone*. When I worked up the nerve to reach out, you shimmered, drifted up like smoke, climbed back into the hole in the ceiling, and all I could think was, *I'm losing you again.*

The mattress squished underfoot as I stood, tried to grab on to your foot before you were out of reach. You disappeared into your hole, quick as a spider, turned back to smile at me, and reach back a hand, fingers splayed and sticky with honey light.

And your music was so loud, so true. It covered me in a way it hadn't since your death. Like every breath and every note was for me.

The outside world, hardened, froze, and I knew it was just you and me there, listening, choosing what kind of eternity we wanted. I knew in that moment, if I took your hand and let you lift me up, I could live in your music forever.

Follow me, golden empty, find me where I lead.

I hesitated, and I still don't know why. It would have been so easy.

You watched me lie back on my bed, grinned and shook your head as if to say you had your chance, then you were nothing but a poster on my celling again. My eyes became heavy, and the drug drew me down to sleep, but all those voices continued to echo around the room, calling on me, taunting me, begging me to climb out of my miserable life and join the mystery.

It wasn't the worst idea I'd ever heard.

✱

I was addicted to the music. Addicted to you. And the graveweed brought you close again, every time I smoked it. Sometimes you sat at the foot of my bed, strumming a guitar. Other times, it was just your face, wild and pulsing like a living heart, peering down from the hole in the ceiling, your backing band a chorus of unseen singers. To my mind, they were ghosts. They sang the music of the dead, songs that were written ages ago, songs too beautiful to ever be sung by the living.

The music, that's why April had been so excited for me to smoke the graveweed. She understood me.

She knew it would blow my mind.

Marcus called them aural hallucinations, but I don't know if that's even a real thing. Everybody who smoked graveweed heard some kind of music, though, and everybody had a hallucinatory visit from somebody they missed. Dead grandma, or your best friend who died in elementary school. April said she saw her beagle, Sparks, that got hit by a car when she was ten. Everybody loved the shit out of it, but the difference with me was, I knew it was more than a vision. Or it was for me at least. You were *real*. You were dead, but you'd come back for me.

Anyway, the graveweed became popular.

Who doesn't want to be high on music?

And those ghost songs began to rewire my brain—they made me hungry, reckless, less afraid of death. The dead, they wanted me to sing along. They wanted me to join you in the afterlife, but no matter how much I wanted that myself, I was too afraid to follow.

Still, I felt like I was working my way up to it.

I came close one night, standing on my bed, arms reaching up to see if it was even possible to climb through to you. Hobie opened my door, no knock, just walked in and saw me there with honey oozing down my arms and my eyes reflecting moonlight from the afterlife. But here's the thing, guys like Hobie are never going to know *real* magic when they see it; they don't understand how you can love something so much that it can fracture the world, change what reality means. All guys like Hobie are going to see is their girlfriend's psycho daughter dancing on her bed and laughing at the ceiling, and that's okay, because what I was seeing, I'd never want to share that with him.

"The fuck you doing?" he said. "Your mom has dinner ready. She's been calling you."

"*See behind my black heart, I see behind yours.*" I'm not sure if I responded to him myself, or if it was you singing through me, but I knew all the words to "Black Heart" like they were sewn into my soul.

"Are you high or something?" he asked.

I started humming the melody.

"Are you smoking pot?" he asked.

I shook my head. "Nope." It was the truth.

"I don't care what you do, but your mother wants your ass at the dinner table."

She didn't want me at the dinner table. She just wanted to play out her ideal of the normal family that she'd never managed to cultivate, and there was no understudy to take my place. I laughed at Hobie, nurturing that dark notion that all teenagers cling to at one time or another—*maybe something will happen to me, maybe I'll die, and then you'll be sorry.* But my laughter faded when I realized he wouldn't be sorry. I wasn't even sure Mom would care. If I went missing like one of these milk carton kids, would she bother to look for me? In the years since we left Texas, she'd made it clear that everything had been okay between her and my dad until I came along. Like I'd cracked open the good egg he'd been and let all the violence come pouring out. And if that meant I brought out the violence in her sometimes too, I need only look in the mirror to find who was at fault.

Lift your black heart, look underneath, is that me?

Fuck, a lyric for everything, I guess.

"What's your deal, kid?" he asked.

"No deal." I sung the words, like I was singing "Black Heart." "Tell Mom I'm coming."

"Snap to it," he said, then left me alone with you.

My high was fading, and the portal absorbed your soul again, sealed you away. I was out of graveweed, which meant after dinner I had to go see my least favorite drug dealer.

At the table, Mom asked probing questions about boys and drugs—I'm sure Hobie told her I was acting like a freak again—but I just hummed and chewed my macaroni casserole while they stabbed at their food and grew irritated. Afterward, none of us were in the mood to clean up. Hobie found a basketball game on the television and Mom sat across the table from me, dumping her after dinner cigarette ash into her empty plate, a ritual that always turned my stomach.

"You need to be nicer to Hobie," she said. "He might be your stepdad soon."

"Better than my real dad, I guess."

"Jennifer, you're not as funny as you think," she said. "You're growing up to be a little asshole, and that's not the person you want to be."

"What kind of person do I want to be, Mom?"

"A good one," she said. "One that doesn't make everyone else miserable all the time."

"If you're giving out tips on how to be a good person, I better grab a pen and paper," I said. "I want to make sure and not miss a word of *that* wisdom."

"That's enough. No more out of your mouth."

"You're the one who wanted to talk."

"Jen, I swear to god, you need to shut up."

"What are you going to do?" I asked. "Hit me? Send Hobie into my room to leer while I change into my pajamas?"

"Jennifer!"

"Will you two stop fucking fighting?" Hobie chimed in from the living room like either of us cared.

"You need to tell me what's going on with you."

What did she want me to say? That she was a shitty mom? That her job was to keep me safe, but she put her wants in front of my wellbeing every single time? She knew that, though we played a tug of war with her guilt, Mom trying to stash it somewhere dark and hidden, and me always probing that darkness with a flashlight. I'd given up trying with her, so maybe I deserved what I got, but she'd given up showing any genuine concern for my feelings a long time ago. Like when you died. She knew about it before I did. Heard it on the radio, told me when I got home from school in the same distracted voice she'd use to ask if I was okay with Chinese takeout, or if I had any socks I wanted to toss in with the laundry. *That singer you listen to died in a plane crash outside town. So sad, isn't it?*

That's how little she understood me.

So, yeah, what did she expect me to say?

"Nothing, Mom. I'm going out."

"No way," she said. "Not tonight."

"Yes, tonight. I'm just going for a walk."

"I'm your mother." She spoke the words with authority, as if that simple truth was enough to compel my obedience.

"Yes, you are." I pushed up from the table and headed for the front door, my mother howling behind me to *sit my ass back in the chair*. Hobie stood up like he might try to stand in my way, but we both knew it was bluster. He'd rather see me gone, and Mom was getting exactly what she wanted. A reason to draw all that misery to herself and feel put-upon. She'd been poisoned by self-importance long before I was born.

That was another difference between Mom and me.

I knew from an early age that the world would keep on turning just fine without me in it.

✱

Marcus lived only a few blocks away, and I didn't have a car anyway, so I drew my jacket tight against the wind coming off the bay and started walking. Night moved in, cold and creeping. The last specter of my high gave the streetlights a brittle, starburst look, and ghost music followed me up the street; all those dead voices still sang their songs, they sang *your* songs, and the memory of your voice was a hot whisper in my ear. I started singing along, making up any lyrics I didn't recognize, already feeling like a full-fledged member of the afterlife chorus.

That music had its hooks in my soul.

It wanted to pull me in, and I wanted to let it.

When I reached Marcus's house, I saw April's white Fiero parked out front. She used to take me to school in that little two-seater before Marcus picked up a DUI and lost his license. Now his truck stayed parked at home, and I took the bus. The two of them stood by the car, faces close together and screaming. Marcus was a foot taller than April, and he leaned into her with the weight of his anger, one hand on her bicep, pulling like he was trying to keep her out of the car. I started running, Converse slapping the wet pavement, and when they saw me coming, they flew apart like magnets with the same charge.

"Leave her alone," I said.

"It's okay," said April. "We aren't fighting."

"Bullshit," I said. "Look at you."

April had a bruise up one side of her neck. She'd been crying. Mascara smeared down her cheeks and she drew in every breath like she was at war with the air.

"Why are you at my house, Jennifer?" said Marcus. "You need to go the fuck away."

"Yeah, no. Not by myself anyway. April is leaving with me."

"For real, it's fine," said April.

"This is not *close* to fine."

I'd moved in between April and Marcus without even realizing what I was doing. The ghost song become anxious, aggressive. I could feel the buzz of the music in my back teeth. Marcus put a hand on the car, moved in close to me, and the asshole was smiling. Face flushed red, anger in his breath, but smiling.

"April and me, we're a couple," he said. "Couples fight. But that's between the two of us, and it doesn't involve you at all, no matter how much you maybe wish it did. Do you like me, Jen? Or wait, do you like April? Is that why you're always sticking your nose in our shit?"

"Leave her alone," said April.

"Shut up, okay?" he said. "I asked Jennifer why she's here."

"I just . . . I came for more graveweed."

"Oh, you came because you *needed* something from me."

He wasn't wrong. I felt so lame.

I was desperate to connect with you again. Desperate enough to stand in soggy darkness with a guy who liked to beat up my best friend, hoping he'd sell me enough graveweed to send me chasing after you for good. But I guess there's a kind of strength to be found when you've decided you're better off dying. And I wasn't going to be my mother. I got closer to Marcus, matched his smile, enjoyed the uncertainty in his eyes. Did he grieve anyone enough for them to appear to him in his graveweed haze? Did he hear the music?

Man, I really don't think he did.

"I don't need *shit* from you," I said. "I know where it grows. I'll just go get some myself."

"The fuck you will."

Marcus shoved me into the car so hard, the passenger side window cracked.

April came alive. She grabbed me under my arms, kept me from falling over. Opened the car door and ushered me inside. My back ached, and I wondered if I'd broken a rib. I watched through the smeary windshield as April crossed in front of the car, screaming at Marcus. Words like *psycho* and *we're done* and *keep the fuck away from us*. He dogged her heels, growled obscenities and threats. My adrenaline hadn't quite caught up to the unexpected shock and I felt like I was haunting the edges of reality. The last of my high had fled, and with it, the music. There was nothing to listen to but the urgent sounds of our escape.

April got in behind the wheel, slammed the door.

Hit the LOCK button.

Marcus slapped at the window, then stalked away across his yard, still screaming. April started the car, accelerated away.

"Are you okay?" she asked.

"I think so. Are you?"

April shook her head, tears streaking her face. "No, I'm really not. But I will be. You up for a drive?"

I wasn't up for anything except maybe a trip to the emergency room, but I wasn't about to leave April alone.

"I guess. Where are we going?"

"To the crash site. I figure if Marcus loves that place so much, we might as well burn it to the fucking ground."

✳

April drove us out of town and into the forest.

Both of us were hurting. April had gone over to see Marcus so he could copy her history notes, and somehow even that routine interaction had escalated into a screaming match. As for me, I felt like I'd been kicked in the back by a horse, and I wanted more than ever to escape this whole life. April was still shaking with adrenaline as she turned onto the side road that led to the crash site. She smoked cigarettes and talked hurriedly about how she was really finished with Marcus this time, how she was *so sorry*. I'd heard a lot of this before. She told me she was going to burn down all the graveweed, hit him where it hurts. No more steady cash in his pockets. No more of the notoriety he loved for being the only one with a *connection* to the stuff.

I didn't care what she did. As long as I got enough in my pockets for one more smoke, I was out of there.

I turned on the car stereo, changed it to my favorite station. Cranked it. Band after band that I loved, but none of them sounded the same anymore. The ghost songs took inventory of my desperation. They named my pain. And they'd erased all the things I used to feel about tunes like "Say Hello 2 Heaven" and "Man of Golden Words" and "Lithium." The ghosts had cut out the hearts of those songs and left them dead and bloodless on the ground.

Then one of *your* songs came on the radio.

And yeah, of course it was "Better Be Yours," the lead track off *Sounds like Forever*, because it's exactly what I needed in that moment, and you can always count on the best music to be there for you. That rapid fire snare roll that kicks off the song went colliding into your multi-tracked guitar; two, four, eight guitars all speaking the same language, coming down around us like the sky falling to crush the world. Your voice broke through the chaos, hot with rage, but eager to lift us back up again. This song wasn't dead; this song still had a beating heart. And April, she wasn't talking over the music anymore, she was drumming on the steering wheel with her fingers, singing along with that song that *every single person* from our generation knew like they knew their own name.

Even though I was stone cold sober now, I knew it was you telling me I was on the right path.

When the song ended, April parked the car and we trekked into the woods. She led us by the yellow light of the emergency flashlight she kept in her trunk. The clouds hung low and suffocating; they hid every star and held back every ounce of moonlight. But we found the place—*I think you wanted us to find the place*—and there was more graveweed growing than last time, a sprawling and feral patch of the stuff, spilling out from the place you died several yards in all directions. I went down to my knees, plunged my hands into the leaves and felt their warmth. Picked a handful, shoved them in my pockets.

April told me to back up. She thumbed her plastic Bic lighter to life, touched the flame to one of the leaves.

Rain or not, the graveweed was eager to burn.

Those iridescent leaves that had been glistening with moisture the first time I saw them caught fire with the speed of a hardcore drumbeat, and within seconds, we had a full-on bonfire in front of us.

I stared into the flames, wondering idly if the whole state might burn down around us.

But somehow the fire stayed contained to the perimeter of the graveweed growth, as if this was no ordinary fire, but a supernatural conflagration that we'd bound with our fear and our devotion to something much larger than us. Like a summoning circle formed of our fondest desires. The fire shot ten feet in the air, and smoke billowed out thick and sweet and smelling of honey. And that's when Marcus stumbled into the clearing, sweaty and gaping at the bonfire. That's when the flames split down the middle and opened that now familiar gateway to the other side. That's when you stepped out, on fire but not *burning*, and held out your hand to me like a parent telling their child it's time to leave the playground and come home.

I wasn't surprised that Marcus had followed. Suspended license or not, I knew he'd chase us.

Maybe I'd wanted him to?

I breathed deep, took in the smoke, felt my vision blur. Welcomed the rising swell of ghost music that begged me to step through the portal, begged me to die, and promised me death was the answer to every problem I had. You still waited for me, patient and smiling, but you'd grown thin, and your eyes had retreated into your skull. Did you even have eyes? Sharp and crooked bones pressed against the underside of your skin. You looked like a heroin corpse. You kept smiling, but you looked hungry, and I wondered for the first time if this was *really* you.

And if it wasn't you?

Marcus shoved me out of the way, nearly knocked me down. He mumbled under his breath, stood right before you, backlit by angry orange flames.

I have no idea what the graveweed had shown Marcus before, but he was seeing *my* god now. He was hearing *my* music. And he couldn't resist it.

Marcus reached out, tears in his eyes, took your hand.

And you led him through the portal, slow and gentle. Introduced him to the honey light, and gave him everything I'd been dreaming about. Marcus was *there* and then he was gone. His body disappeared; his soul, presumably, joined that haunting forever.

The ghost song rose in volume. You reached your hand out to me again. My fingers hovered close to yours.

Everything could be so, so easy.

Then a hand on my shoulder. April. I could feel the ghost song pulling me close, but her hand kept me in place. She hollered in my ear, raising her voice above the chorus, and she talked about our friendship. She talked about the food fights we used to have in the cafeteria freshman year, and the trips we always made together into Seattle to dig through record stores and dusty used book shops. She talked about all the cool shit we'd do after graduation, like rent a car and drive down to California. We'd stop along the way and take Polaroids of ourselves standing on the cliffs, overlooking the Pacific. We'd load up with junk food and cheap beer and cartons of cigarettes. We'd have the music turned up so loud that it would still ring in our ears hours after we'd turned the stereo off.

And when April felt me still pulling away from her, she started singing "Better Be Yours" again, louder than she'd sung it in the car.

She begged me to *just fucking listen.*

My lips started mouthing the words. The drums became my heartbeat. Your lyrics poured out from my soul. I could hear your song, louder than fear, louder than love, your *real* song, and it silenced the ghosts.

You didn't want me to die, to choose death. You told me that in your lyrics.

Life over death, pain over nothing at all.

It was all right there. You'd been showing me the truth the whole time.

I backed away. April drew me farther from the flames, farther from you. I shook my head—*no, no, no.* Part of me was still afraid I was letting you down.

You stepped back into the portal, peered out at me with that crooked grin that was burned into the memory of a generation.

Then you turned away from me, and you were gone.

April and I huddled together beyond the reach of the bonfire, crying. The orange flames went blue, then green, then died out altogether.

Marcus was gone. The graveweed was gone.

And the world had never seemed so quiet.

✳

That was a long time ago.

Ask most people and they'll say your songs have shed some of their luster and their power over the years. They've been filtered through car commercials and video game soundtracks, covered by top forty artists at Super Bowl halftime shows, been remastered for tenth, twentieth, thirtieth anniversary box sets. And everybody still loves them. No question. But they're just songs to them now, nothing more. Nothing special.

For me, though? Your music resonates more than ever.

But something still gnaws at me. Was that really you, conjured up in the graveweed inferno, or was that something that *looked* like you, hoping to lure me to my death?

Are the dead selfish? Are the dead lonely?

God, I hope not.

I hope when we die, we move beyond all that.

Because here's the thing: some days I can still hear the ghosts. They haunt the static between radio stations, and they fill my long sleepless hours with dark melodies. They assure me you're waiting for me, that you've forgiven my betrayal, that everything I've ever wanted lies just on the other side of this life. I don't want to listen to them, but I can't help myself. And when those voices get loud, I remove the shoebox from the back of my bedroom closet, lift off the lid and touch the bruise-colored leaves within, still as fresh as the day I plucked them from the forest, still slick with thirty-year-old rain. Then I call April, forever my best friend, and she talks me down. She reminds me I have a spouse who loves me, and a pair of bright and beautiful teenagers who need me alive. So, I put the box back on the shelf, even as the ghosts sing louder, knowing that it's always there, and understanding deep in my soul that someday I won't have the willpower left in me to resist it.

When I was a kid, I fell in love with your music, and it broke my heart.

But I forgive you.

And one day I'm going to give us a second chance.

THEIR BLOOD SMELLS OF LOVE AND TERROR

I don't want the things they offer me.

Warm blood and broken skulls. Grunting pigs and headless roosters. Bottles of cold milk I can't drink and hard bread I can't eat. There's only one thing I really want, and none of them is likely to give it to me.

I'm tired, and I want to finish dying.

Night sits heavy against the harvested fields as my bones stir beneath the soil. They find one another, grind together, and take shape as I inhabit that old skin and prepare to play my part once again. Summer is dead. The people who work this land have gathered to pay for their prosperity, and it's my responsibility to collect. I'd gladly recede into the gray gloom that has long been denied me and forgive them the debt.

But it's hard to overcome the legend.

I greet them wearing a wrinkled brown suit and a crooked string tie. Shoes dusty and dull, with the soles pulling away. I carry an oak-handled scythe, a tool I don't require, but the people expect a certain image from a creature like me. My dress and my manner evoke their grandfathers and stern guidance. I am a touchstone, linking them with every harvest going back before the days of oxen and plow, to the time when we used sticks to dig and turn the soil. My straw hat is warped and muddy. My face is a terror, patterned in gray and brown scales, with a jaw that unhinges wide enough to take a child's head into my mouth and draw the life from her with my fangs.

The people wait on bended knee.

I had hoped they'd finally reject me, but their misplaced faith appears intact.

When I leave the empty fields and walk along the town's lone paved street, I'm met with a bounty. Golden stalks of wheat bent into geometric shapes so ancient the people have forgotten their original meaning. Tin buckets of fresh blueberries and fat Mason jars filled with honeycombs. A spotted calf lies in my path, flayed open from neck to groin, as if I have any interest in such a thing. I step over the bloody body and hiss a note of displeasure. At the very least, they might spare some miserable beast next year. Pecan shells crack beneath my steps, and I scatter corn husks and field mouse bones with my scythe as I proceed to the town square.

The town stands in the shadows of twin grain silos, built of weathered brown bricks, capped with conical roofs. The windows of the pharmacy advertise headache powders and vanilla ice cream sodas. A corrugated aluminum building houses a diesel cotton gin. Many of my worshipers traveled from their homes in motorcars or on sputtering green tractors. They live in a world of miracles but still can't slough off the old ways, no matter how painful a burden they've become for us all.

Their blood smells of love and terror, and it's such a heady thing, I take a deep breath. The adoration makes me weak, and I must remind myself I'm not a god.

There was no god when I was killed, and there is no god now.

There is just a hungry eternity.

The sacrifice is named Eliza and she's fourteen years old. The men usher her forward and toss her to the ground at my feet. They retreat in a rush, more afraid of me than the girl is.

Eliza wears a sackcloth dress, and someone has shaved her head bald for the ceremony. She holds a wilted sprig of cotton in her small hands, like a bridal bouquet, and a cottonmouth snake skull is tied to it with a bit of blue ribbon. The skull's empty eye sockets are meant to gaze upon the brightest possible future for the town. The teeth symbolize the bite of death, necessary payment for continued prosperity.

I look over my worshipers and absorb their fear. Any one of them could raise a rifle and shoot me down. They could converge and overpower me, take my own scythe, cut off my head. And I would let them. It's only their belief and their tiresome superstitions that keep us locked in this cycle, and no matter how hard I try, I can't seem to upset it.

I offer my cold hand to Eliza, and she takes it.

We know one another well now.

Every year I lie uneasy in my half grave, wet and tangled in the roots, and I listen to everyone moving above me, alert to every fret and folly that plagues the town. And I do my best to guide them, though they rarely pay attention. I whisper my counsel in their dreams, but they close their minds to my words. They hear me, but they don't want to *listen*. They only think they want a god.

I help Eliza to her feet, and she looks right into my yellow eyes. She recognizes me from her dreams, and I wonder if she remembers what I've told her. What I've begged her to do. *Refuse me. I am not your god. I am only a corpse. I hold no sway over your lives or your prosperity.*

The town holds its breath, so quiet I can hear cattle lowing from a fenced-in pasture beyond the fields. The people have dimmed their harsh electric bulbs for my sake; barn lanterns and smoky tallow candles light the proceedings. I've called this place home for so many decades, I've lost count. We hadn't even the dream of electric lights when I was full of youth, and the night then was a deep and terrible thing these people could never conceive.

Despite their attempts to hold it at bay, the darkness hardens around us with the weight of ritual.

Eliza holds my gaze, and I wonder if she's seeing the monster or my real face. I used to be a young girl with sun-browned skin and bleeding calluses on my hands, living through a drought that promised never to end, and my people, my *family*, buried me alive in the fields, hoping my blood would water the soil and appease a deity that didn't exist. Cottonmouth snakes burrowed in close against my skin, cold and corrupt. Beetles and June bugs nestled inside my rib cage and chewed away my vitals. Rain eventually poured down and seeped into my grave as my teeth fell loose and my skin pulled away from my bones. And I remained in the earth for the entire year, listening to the afterlife call me, begging whatever force kept me there in the ground to let me die. When summer collapsed into fall again, I dug my way out and became the thing they wanted to see. The god they wanted to fear. Brother Fang. Old Cottonmouth. So many names, but they all mean the same thing. I am the keeper of the harvest, without whom they would all starve and die.

Every year I rise, and every year they feed their young women to me. Always their young women.

The people are afraid to move, but I can feel the motion of their hearts and the tension in their backs. They're wondering if I'll find Eliza worthy, as if anyone can be judged worthy or not for such a reason.

Oak leaves ride the breeze, and the air smells like animal sweat and dried dung. I breathe in all that life despite myself. These sensations aren't meant for me, but I can't help but mourn the life I used to have. Eliza doesn't flinch when I cup her bald head with my talon. Most of them do. My jaws open wide to reveal the white membrane within and curved fangs wet with venom. I can't help the hunger I feel, the need to accept the people's sacrifice. If it were as simple as refusing to feed, I'd gladly starve and die. But long ago I realized it's their belief in my power that binds me here, and I simply can't resist.

I wish I could hate them all for it, but I understand their desperation.

We have spoken in dreams many times, but now I place a question into Eliza's waking thoughts. *Do you offer yourself willingly for the harvest? For the good of the town? For all who gather now, and all who come after?*

I've prepared her for this moment. Begged her to release me from their worship. I have drawn her mind down into the soil and shown her its secrets.

But Eliza stands before me, eyes bright and ready to die.

The old people caution their children from an early age not to believe what I tell them. I may be their god, but I am, after all, a serpent. I cannot convince this town their prosperity has nothing to do with whether I'm pleased or angered. I'm neither of these things, only sad and tired and eager to escape.

Eliza has not given her answer, has not voiced her assent, a necessary part of the ritual we've unwittingly built. The town fathers rumble low in their throats and risk dark glances in her direction. This is not uncommon. The sacrifice often hesitates and must be coaxed to speak.

But Eliza is smiling, and this is something I've never seen before.

I repeat my question. *Do you offer yourself willingly for the harvest? For the good of the town? For all who gather now, and all who come after?*

Eliza shakes her head, answers aloud.

"No. I'm sorry. No."

And that is all it takes.

The afterlife opens before me like a flower greeting spring sunshine, irresistible and golden.

Then I'm gone, and nothing remains in my place but a wind-tossed pile of bone dust and a dry, transparent snakeskin coiled around a brown suit and battered shoes. My scythe blade blows away, a cloud of rust, and the shaft clatters against the brick street. My essence, my soul if you want to call it that, hovers overhead, already dissolving into whatever comes next, and Eliza looks up and keeps smiling as if she can still see me there.

I think maybe she can.

For the first time in ages, I feel something like joy.

I'm no longer bound to the earth by superstition and human weakness. Eliza has chosen life, the only blessing I can ever bestow, and she's given me the final death I've been begging for.

A woman wails from the crowd, and someone screams an obscenity. The town rises as one. None of them can see me anymore.

They see only the girl who killed their god.

There is no hesitation. The people fall upon Eliza with splintered axe handles and heavy fists. She resists with open palms and spindly arms, but there are too many. Work boots stomp and rusty pocketknives stab. Eliza screams until her voice falters. The stench of the town's anger and fear pollutes the air, and I want to let go, to allow death to absorb what remains of me, but someone must bear witness. The people are driven by a fear older than themselves, and while I don't believe they understand what truly motivates them, they are terrified to reveal any faithlessness.

Eliza's own parents go at her the hardest, as if to distance themselves from her sin.

If I were truly a god, I'd strike them all dead.

Eliza lies in the street. Bones protrude like jagged tree limbs, and her eyes are swollen shut, but she is still alive. Crawling. I wish I could reach out and take her hand. I want to assure her that death is close, and not so terrible, but I don't know that for certain. Eliza moans through broken teeth, scrapes her hands and knees against the gravel in a frantic effort to escape. This cannot be the end of her. Eliza is a girl who loves running barefoot though wet grass on summer nights, capturing fireflies in glass jars, listening for owl calls and the rustle of night winds through the brush. She collects porcelain dolls and sleeps with a blind old terrier named Samuel, whom she's known her whole life and treasures above all other creatures. She is smart and curious and, yes, sometimes willful. She knew there would be a cost for her defiance.

But she had not expected *this*. Neither of us had.

We were both fools.

One of the town fathers sweeps Eliza up in his arms like she's a sack of cornmeal and tosses her onto a flatbed trailer attached to a tractor.

The people watch, eyes glassy and afraid.

The tractor shudders to life, chokes out oily black smoke, and lurches forward, pulling the trailer behind it. The people follow, marching up the street and into the fields, parishioners in a cursed congregation. Their procession is silent and gilded with shame, and their faith draws them through the darkness to a place none of them really wants to go.

There is already a hole. A grave. My home.

The tractor goes silent, and the night becomes a web of fevered whispers, raspy breathing, and quiet sobs. The same man who loaded Eliza onto the trailer lowers her into the hole. Her chest still rises and falls, but there's not much life left inside her. What remains of my spirt hovers overhead like a gray storm cloud as the people converge to bury her alive. They shovel in handfuls of dirt, eager to cover her up before she opens her eyes. I wonder for the first time if there was another girl before me, if there will be more after Eliza, if there was ever a time when these people were not so afraid of the world that they turned their daughters into gods.

It seems the people must have *someone* to worship, but I can't let someone else take on that burden, else I'd be no better than they are.

I flow like cold moonlight through the soil and take up residence inside Eliza's body. This despite the hungry pull of the afterlife, so eager to have me that I need only relent for one second to become part of the mystery. But I can't let this girl take my place. It's easy enough for me to jostle her spirit loose and send it skyward. She's newly dead, and I've far more experience walking the tricky path between now and forever. She rises from her own chest like smoke from a chimney, hangs above us all in a moment of terrible clarity. We see one another, and she understands what I've done. What remains of the girl Eliza used to be smiles down at me.

Then the universe inhales, and breathes her in.

I'm alone inside the body now, feeling every broken bit of my new self, feeling the weight of the soil layered on my chest. I catch a momentary glimpse of the haunted, sweaty people peering into my grave before the dirt fills my gasping mouth and covers my eyes. Already I can hear the burrowing approach of the things that will remake this corpse, but I'm not afraid.

I've been here before.

When my breathing goes entirely still and the people are gone, I invite the corruption back in. Even as I wonder what form I'll wear when I rise next year, I realize it doesn't matter. I could be Old Cottonmouth, or the town's imagination could conjure up a new, more fearsome god.

No amount of blood can water the furrows.

No amount of grief can make the wheat grow taller.

And I pray to whatever god will listen that one day they'll all figure that out.

A RED PROMISE IN THE PALM OF YOUR HAND

I clasp my hands in prayer as Mr. Amos sews wings onto my dead brother's shoulders. Mr. Amos approaches his task with care. He works the catgut thread in and out of Robert's skin, pulling every stitch taut. He is carrying out God's plan, though I'm not sure what god he means anymore. We abandoned our Christian god sometime back, just as the Christian god abandoned us.

So claims Mr. Amos, in any event.

This is wrong, Bess.

Mother's voice again. She is two years dead, but her spirit remains. This clapboard house is her living corpse. The wind presses against the walls and gives her breath. She speaks through groaning timbers and the door clattering in its broken frame.

In the evenings, wind rushes down through the stone chimney and becomes her screams.

These creatures fly in the face of creation.

Mother sounds bitter, but that doesn't necessarily mean she's wrong.

"Bess. Help me, please?" Mr. Amos waves me over, bites off the thread with an eye tooth, fastens the last knot. "Get his feet, if you would."

Mr. Amos wears dusty black pants and a once-white shirt, now a ruin of brown stains. His eyes are sunk deep into his sun-red face, but they forever skip across the surface of the world like a flat stone on a lake, never still. He chews at a matchstick, rolling it back and forth between his teeth.

Mr. Amos grabs Robert's torso, I lift his legs, and together we haul him outside. His small body is easy enough to move, even with its new appendages.

The stone waits for us, black with old blood, an upcropping of flat granite in the rough shape of a triangle, about ten feet long. Mr. Amos said this stone table was a holy place for the Comanches, but we have lived here on the edge of the Llano since Robert was a baby, and we've never seen a Comanche. Mother believed they were frightened of this place. Mr. Amos is confident the new god we've brought with us into the wilderness keeps any outsiders at bay.

I'm no longer certain if we brought our god with us or if He was here already, waiting.

We position Robert on the stone table and Mr. Amos stands back, hands on his hips.

"I envy that boy," he says. "Those are good wings."

Robert lies on his back and the wings fan out on either side, each of them three feet long. They're crafted of mesquite limbs and animal hides, rib bones and clay. I helped Mr. Amos with their creation. If my brother was to die, I intended for him to have the finest wings I could provide.

"Your mother would be proud of her beautiful boy."

My mother has told me what she thinks of this, but I'm the only one who still hears her. Or maybe the only one who listens.

"It's getting close to dark," I say.

The sun sits fat and red against the horizon. Long shadows grow from the row of houses, situated in an arc around the stone table. Loose boards rattle, and the roofs have been torn away from the houses that used to belong to the Lancasters and the Hendersons. Our empty stock pen is a mess of leaning mesquite pickets and overgrown scrub brush. The wind stalks the flat earth. Used to be we cared for this home we built for ourselves, but there have been too few of us left to do that for a long time.

I know we can't be out here after dark, but I need another moment with my brother. I comb his hair with my fingers, moving it out of his eyes. He's cold despite the late summer heat, and his skin is already growing gray and bloated. His body yawns red from chest to stomach, and the bloody knife that made the killing cut hangs from Mr. Amos's belt. I don't feel the kind of anguish I've been expecting, but then again, I've been mourning Robert since before his death.

"Let's go, Bess," Mr. Amos says. "Don't want to get caught out after dark."

No, we definitely do not want to get caught out.

*

We butchered the last of our pigs earlier in the summer and now Mr. Amos and I finish off the shank with a side of snap peas and hard bread. We dine from the remnants of Mother's china, brought with us from Austin—red roses faded to pink, gold gilt chipping away from the edges. The china was handed down from her grandmother, and it was the only thing Mother insisted on bringing with us, no matter how impractical. Mr. Amos encouraged every one of us to release our worldly possessions before we set off into the wilderness. And so, we had, save for that china.

"We shall both follow young Robert, whither he goes." Mr. Amos attempts to smile, but it's weighed down by his gray mustache. "You and I will find glory too."

We both know Mr. Amos is too old to follow. Where he will go when he passes is a mystery.

God only gives flight to the young.

"If I'm the next chosen to serve, my killing will be up to you," he says. "Your hands must be quick, and they must be steady. You're a faithful girl. You'll be up to the task."

There used to be so many of us living in this wilderness. Now it's just Mr. Amos and me. I've given no thought to what will happen if I am the last of us alive. My only concern is whether our god will accept me if I'm chosen. I am nearly seventeen and there is some question as to whether I'm a child or an adult. No adult in our community has ever been granted flight. Now the possibility of outliving everyone else burns in my mind like a fever.

Kill him before he kills you. Do it tonight.

I ignore my mother's voice and clear away the dishes while Mr. Amos ensures every window is shuttered, the door firmly barred. The wind beats against the house, causing it to groan and shriek, and since the wind never relents, neither do my mother's admonishments.

Listen to me, Bess. They're monsters.

Every shuddering board gives her voice, and she grows louder as darkness falls.

We were wrong to come here. I'm sorry.

I wash the dishes while Mr. Amos sits in a low chair by the fire, rolling a cigarette. The bone jar sits on the roughhewn cedar mantle, a heavy thing made of murky green glass and filled with rib bones we all collected from the land. The bones are sun-whitened and brittle, save for one stained red with blood. It waits there for each of us, like eternity. Just as cold and just as uncertain. Robert was the last one to pull the red bone from the jar, and soon enough Mr. Amos and I will gather around it and take our turns again.

Mr. Amos smokes his cigarette and retires early to his bed, as is his habit. I situate myself in his vacated chair by the fire and listen for them to arrive.

It would be no sin to drive the carving knife into his chest while he sleeps.

Once, Mother was the most devout of us all, but she lost her faith. I'm not sure what to believe anymore. Only Mr. Amos remains to guide me in matters of the spirt, and his gospel now carries the taint of desperation.

I hear heavy wings in flight, then something thumps against the roof. This pattern is repeated until I count at least seven of the fliers on our roof, and many more in the yard. In my mind they circle Robert, eager to receive him. They are angels with golden halos and mournful eyes. Their soft hands lift my brother's body and urge him to flight.

Mr. Amos snores from his sleeping loft, his rest aided by a dram of whisky.

I'm wide awake.

Mother has gone quiet, thinking perhaps they won't remember her. This ploy is never effective.

Right away, the fliers on our roof begin to pick at the shingles, hammering with hands and feet and wings. Others batter the walls, loosening the clapboard siding. All of this elicits a scream from my mother that makes me question everything I've been taught.

Why did she abandon her beliefs? Why did she abandon Robert and me? Her miserable afterlife is her own fault, and yet that doesn't keep me from mourning her sad state.

This commotion carries on for several minutes, and then the fliers are gone as quickly as they came. Mother's screams continue for most of the night.

She is my mother, so I listen, and try not to judge.

*

We spend the next morning pretending at normal life.

There are no animals left to be tended, but there are weeds to be pulled from the garden and water to be hauled from the nearby creek. Mr. Amos climbs onto the roof with a hammer and nails, working to undo the damage from the night before. His efforts are pointless. He labors against the inevitable. The house can never be what it was, and what is repaired will only be pulled apart again. The fliers will rend Mother's spirit just as they did her body. But to Mr. Amos, the house is nothing more than shelter, and the work keeps him busy. He's a man quickly running out of purpose, and it would be cruel to take anything else away from him.

Robert's body is gone from the stone table. I place my hands where we'd laid him, and the rock is hot to the touch. I consider what it will feel like to be left there. To open my eyes to the afterlife with all my friends eager to accept me.

I move about my tasks in a malaise, muddled by lack of sleep and wishing for the time when there were others to share the labor.

Thirteen families founded this community. Seventy-four people in all, including my mother, my brother, and me. My father passed not long after Robert was born, and his death broke Mother. It was Mr. Amos who seemingly put her together again, with his sermons about the failure of our old religion and the promise of the new. And when they took up together in a family away, his whole congregation celebrated. It was Mother's decision as much as his for all of us to leave Austin and build a life someplace beyond the reach of human judgement. When I was little more than a toddler, we all rode out together, and kept going until Mr. Amos found the stone table and assured us we had reached our Eden.

Paradise proved to be hot and dusty and difficult, but this place was ours, and we were all glad to have it. No matter the cost.

Everything according to His plan.

Late in the morning I call Mr. Amos off the roof for a glass of water. We stand together in the shade of the covered porch, both of us withered by the summer heat. Age has whittled him down to bones and his long hair has gone gray.

We share in the silence. I miss the slow, struggling whine of the windmill, its mechanism now seized up and several of its blades rusting in the tall yellow weeds. A plow languishes in the field. I miss the good-natured chatter of families working toward a shared goal. Quails used to scamper through the brush, and mockingbirds called from the trees, but even they have left this place. And while the mesquites and sticker burrs and other hard things still cling to the cracked earth, everything worth loving here has long since blown away.

Everything is dying, as if the land itself ushers us toward our inevitable conclusion.

"God be good. They accepted him into the fold." Mr. Amos motions with his glass to the empty stone table.

"Robert was always a faithful child." I recite the words he expects from me, though I'm not sure Robert was old enough to understand that kind of faith.

"That he was. And smart as a whip, too." Mr. Amos makes a sharp face as he bites back the alkaline taste of the water. "That boy could light up your mother's eyes. She loved him so." Talk of Mother clouds his expression with sadness, and he shakes his head, like he's trying to dislodge bad memories.

"Yes, she was fond of him," I say. "She loved us all, but I think Robert was her special one."

Mr. Amos smiles. "Might be he was."

"Mr. Amos, I feel some uncertainty."

"We're every one of us uncertain. That's why faith is so necessary."

"I think what I mean to say is, I'm not prepared for this. Maybe I'll be chosen first, but the Lord could call for you next and then I'll be by myself."

"That is a possibility."

"Who'll sew my wings when it's my time?"

"The Lord will provide," he says.

"Is there any other course of action we might take? Some way both of us could live. With His blessing, of course. Must we carry this through to the end?"

Mr. Amos has been watching a bit of dust spin up and dance along the horizon, but my words sharpen his attention, and he puts a leathery hand on my shoulder like he's afraid I might bolt.

"There is no other path to walk. Don't go looking for one."

My mother went looking for one. The fliers found her, brought her body back in pieces, and left it in the yard.

"I wouldn't," I say. "I won't."

"We'll carry on as we always have. And this will end as we've always known it would."

The big knife never leaves Mr. Amos's hip; it lives there as a promise about exactly how this will end.

"Yes sir, I suppose it will."

Mr. Amos hands me his glass and climbs back onto the roof. The sound of his hammer echoes through the afternoon. When he comes back down for dinner, he reveals the Lord's command.

We're drawing bones tonight.

✳

In the evening, we place the bone jar between us on the dining table and plunge our hands inside, removing the bones, one by one. We close our eyes as we draw. We open them to reveal if one of us has chosen the red bone, or if we must draw again.

The drawing of bones used to be a festive event in our community, one accompanied by laughter and good food. Chicken and potatoes with butter. Fried okra and pies with freshly harvested pecans. All of us gathered around in anticipation as Mr. Keller played his guitar and sang godly songs. Whether we drew our bones in the dusty sunlight with cicadas in chorus around us or beneath gray clouds, earth dusted with snow, the bone jar held a ceremonial position on the stone table. All of us surrounding it, taking our turns, until the selection of one soul was met with joy, and a measure of hidden sadness. A tightness always came to my chest. I'd close my eyes and breathe slowly, catching the smell of juniper and wildflowers on the breeze, and I was never certain whether to feel disappointed or quietly happy that I hadn't been chosen.

I still can't say which was right.

Over time, our numbers dwindled, and I began to wonder whether His most devout servants were taken first, or if He left the best of us for last.

Maybe our god wouldn't take everyone.

Then the fliers hunted down my mother, and I knew that none of us were leaving here by any method other than His.

Mr. Amos and I have no energy left for fanfare. Tonight, we eat cold dried beef and hard biscuits. We draw the bones not beneath the summer sky, but by the uncertain light of a guttering candle.

Mr. Amos appears upset about our earlier conversation. It's not the first time I've prodded at the edges of our faith, but never so overtly. He approaches our ceremony in workmanlike fashion, opening his eyes to reveal each bloodless bone in his hand, then tossing it to the floor with a grunt. He's going at the whisky harder than is his nature, and it clouds his eyes. If he has a preference whether he lives or dies, it's impossible to tell.

When the jar is half empty and the oak floorboards are littered with rib bones, one of us is finally chosen.

I open my eyes, and there it is. A red promise in the palm of my hand.

Mr. Amos stares at the bone, his mouth slightly open. His breathing is raspy, like something coarse is trying to escape his throat. He washes it back with whisky from the bottle and finds his words.

"It'll be you then."

Run away, Bess!

Mr. Amos turns his head, listens. Like he's hearing her for the first time. Decides it's only the wind.

You'll be damned if you let him gut you. You'll be one of them.

I am damned already, whether she sees that or not. That choice was made the moment we rode out from Austin.

"Do you need help with your wings?" Mr. Amos asks.

I shake my head, still holding the red bone.

I can build them myself.

✳

I spend most of the next day building my wings.

They are not so grand as the ones I made for Robert. Stiff leather lashed to a frame of rusted baling wire. A few chicken feathers and some mesquite bark. They will function, perhaps, but they're not beautiful.

Mr. Amos busies himself with any task he can find. He's stopped speaking to me, and I'm not certain what's happening in his mind. My own thoughts center on his knife parting my breastbone, and his methodical hands working at my back with hammer and awl, like a saddle maker. When he places my body on the stone table, will the fliers come for me like they have all the other children, or will I be harshly judged?

Will they recognize me as a child at all?

This question consumes me as the afternoon shadows grow long and Mr. Amos takes a seat on the front porch, sharpening his knife against a whetstone.

Every one of us is given wings and offered to Him on the stone table, but only children are blessed with flight. When the night grows dark and the living have barricaded themselves inside our homes, the fliers bleed new life into the children and lift them up among their number. The adults, in their hubris, all believe they are faithful enough to join these angels. But every one of them is torn asunder. Their new wings are shredded. Little remains of them but blood and a few bones.

I haul my wings inside our home. Mr. Amos offers me a nod when I pass. The steady rasp of his knife against the stone counts down the seconds of my life.

Mother's voice is sullen. *Stupid girl.*

I place my wings carefully in the corner and take a seat in one of the dining chairs. "My choices aren't what brought us here."

You could have left.

The lie is so bold that I don't bother responding.

I tried my best. I love you.

"You tried to leave, and you didn't take us with you. You didn't even tell us you were going."

Your stepfather's faith is fierce. I was too afraid.

"Are you afraid now?" I asked. "When the fliers come?"

Yes.

"When I'm a flier, I'll pick at your bones too."

"Who are you talking to?" Mr. Amos stands in the doorway.

"My mother."

His face wrinkles up, unsure what to make of this. A few seconds later, he thinks he has it sorted, and he nods his head. "It's good to pray."

"I'm a faithful girl."

"Bess, we'll need to get on with this now, if I'm to finish the work before nightfall."

He might as well be talking about whitewashing the siding or digging a few postholes for all the emotion he reveals. I remember the quiet way he reassured Robert at the end, the way he calmed him by humming one of the old hymns. Robert was resolute, right up until the moment Mr. Amos drew his knife, and then I had to hold my brother tight to keep him from running. That knife tore a wet scream loose from Robert's lungs.

The sound still haunts me.

Mr. Amos walks closer, and there's no one to hold me in place. I stand and scamper away. Terror gnaws at the structure of my faith.

"I don't think I'm ready, Mr. Amos."

"Our day is chosen for us," he says. "The decision is not ours."

Kill him!

"I don't want to," I say.

Mr. Amos unsheathes his knife.

"It'll be okay, Bess. I swear by the love I have for you children and for your mother that I'll do this quick. You won't suffer none."

Wind crashes from the west and Mother rages. Her words become incoherent. Her will is immaterial. The heat of death suffuses her corpse, and I want nothing more right now than to escape from inside her. If I could wish myself into never having been born, I'd make that choice in an instant, but there is not enough love or faith remaining in the world to compel me toward my own death.

In the end, my fear wins out.

I back myself up against the stone fireplace as Mr. Amos advances. He whispers words of comfort that I cannot hear over Mother's anger. The bone jar waits there on the mantle. Useless now. There will never be another drawing. Mr. Amos will most likely die a lonely old man, forever wondering why he was the last of us.

He slides the rocking chair out of the way, close enough now that I can smell last night's whisky.

His lips grasp at prayers.

Mr. Amos clenches his jaw and the wiry muscles in his neck grow taut beneath the stubble of his beard. He tries to get a hand on me, to hold me still, but he doesn't expect a real fight.

I reach for the bone jar, heft it over my head. The green glass is thick and heavy. When I bring it down against his face with everything I have, Mr. Amos drops like he's been shot.

The jar slips from my hands, shatters against the floor. Bones scatter like insects from beneath an overturned rock. Green glass shards swim in the blood that flows like water from the broken dam of Mr. Amos's skull. The right side of his head is a red ruin, and his wide-open eyes are hazy with death. I had no intention of killing him, but I've done it anyway. The walls rattle around me, and Mother's voice stirs up the smell of stale woodsmoke.

I love you. Bess. Please leave. Before they get here.

I can't leave. That much I know.

So, instead, I do what I was raised to do.

❋

I'm sweaty and exhausted by the time I've attached my wings to Mr. Amos's back and dragged his body to the stone table. I whisper prayers over his still form. The old man was faithful to the last, and I hope our god finds him worthy in ways the others were not.

I tell him I'm sorry, but *sorry* solves nothing.

Night crowds in from all sides. Wind whistles through the carcass of what used to be our community. A year or two after we're all gone, the wilderness will have reclaimed every inch. All the meat, all the life, chewed away. None of us will even be a memory. I wonder what our life here has been for, and I suppose that is where our faith must provide the answers, but when our spirits have fled and even the fliers have abandoned this place, who'll be left to care? I sit on the stone table beside Mr. Amos, losing myself in this melancholy, until I hear a sound like storm winds tossing a mainsail, and I know the fliers are close.

I slide down off the stone table and run to our house.

Inside, Mother shrieks, but I no longer listen to what she says. She has failed me, but in these last desperate moments I have decided not to fail her. I won't endure another night of her soul being twisted and torn. If I'm to leave this place, which I mean to do one way or another, I won't abandon her. I won't let her insides fill up with rats and horned toads and muddy wasp nests. She won't face eternity here alone.

I rummage through the pantry until I find the canister of kerosene on the bottom shelf. In half a minute, the table, the chairs, the blue lace curtains, the old rocker, are all doused with the stuff. I don't know where my mother's soul will end up when this house is gone, but it can't be a worse hell than the one she's burning in now.

I strike a kitchen match. I light the whole box.

When I leave the house and slam the door behind me, Mother is already engulfed.

Wings thunder overhead, and I don't bother to hide. I spent so much time wondering if the fliers would have me, that I never considered what might happen if I was chosen and refused to die. Now my fate is no more certain than my mother's. No more certain than that of poor Mr. Amos.

If they mean to punish me, I surely deserve it.

The ground shakes as they land all around me, my angels. They crawl about on hands and feet, sniffing at the earth. Faces of bone, bodies gone gray, red tongues tasting the air. Their wings stir the smoke that billows from the burning house. A few of them whisper back and forth in a language I can't decipher. They have no interest in Mr. Amos. Instead, they grab me with bent fingers and pull me to my knees. There are so many. I should be afraid, but I'm not.

I know these children. They're all my friends.

Robert crouches before me. His eyes are black holes, but his little boy smile is the same as it's always been. He offers me his hand, and I take it without reservation. Pain cuts a trail up my spine and settles in my shoulder blades. The bones in my back bend and snap and shudder. They press against my insides, looking for a way to escape.

When my wings come, my screams are joyful.

The rest of them close in. So cold. So beautiful.

And we rise together, into the heavens.

WE SHARE OUR RAGE WITH THE RIVER

My father and I rode down to the river with Ellis, so we could help fetch him a wife. There had come a hard rain the night before, and the Brazos was angry. I had a notion that if I got too close, the river would swallow me and carry my bones to the sea. I was ten years old and convinced all manner of mysterious creature lurked beneath the roiling brown waters. Despite my fear, I had a yearning to swim out there and find out for myself.

Maybe to keep swimming and never come back.

We dismounted, boots sinking into the mud along the bank. I helped lash the horses to cottonwood trees so they wouldn't spook. My father, my older brother Ellis, and a few of the other men waded out into the river, unravelling fishing nets behind them. The Brazos wasn't deep along this stretch, but the rains made the river violent. Father shouted commands, waist deep and struggling against the current.

Mr. Bolton and a couple of the other men from the settlement remained with me on shore. They held long ropes that had been tied off to the nets, ready to pull. Mr. Bolton's shirtsleeves were rolled up, and his trousers were tucked into tall leather boots. Like all of us, he was ripe with sweat, feeling the humid air all the way to his bones. The brim of his hat drooped forward, but not enough to hide the hungry expression he wore as he watched the others fan out across the river.

The horses whickered; their hooves punched the earth.

They wanted no more to do with this than I did.

Mr. Bolton looked up, saw me comforting one of the mares with my hand on her mane.

"Don't worry, boy," he said. "We won't be here long. Water running wild like this stirs them river women up into a frenzy. They'll be on the move. No better time to catch a wife than right after a hard rain."

He wasn't wrong.

We'd been there no more than ten minutes when everyone started shouting. Out in the middle of the river, one of the nets jumped. Something big splashed about, frothing the surface of the river. Part of me wondered, maybe hoped, that they'd found a knot of water moccasins, but I knew better. My father shouted and the rope in Mr. Bolton's hand went taut.

"Get to pulling!" Mr. Bolton heaved, and the others joined in.

I stood beside the two-wheeled cart we'd brought to haul our catch back to town. I felt like running, but I'm sorry to admit, my curiosity held me in sway. I watched as they dragged the woman up out of the shallows, bound tight in the net and thrashing. She cut a furrow through the mud as they pulled her toward the cart. Her howls were low and throaty, like a bobcat. The men yelled and laughed and cursed as they wrestled her onto the cart and tied her down. She smelled like turned wet soil. She smelled like lightning storms. Her tail tapered into a heavy fin, and she tried to slap out with it, but the net only drew tighter. I was shocked to see her breasts, something I'd only heard older boys describe, uncovered and drawn in tight against her chest by the netting. Copper colored scales covered her body, bright as polished pennies.

She kept howling. Her mouth was crowded with teeth, slender as sewing needles. Her eyes were liquid gray, like lead poured fresh from a crucible. I could read no expression in those eyes, but I could feel her terror just the same. My breath hitched up in my chest, and my heart was thundering.

It was the first time I'd seen a river woman before she changed, and I fought back against the warm tears forming in my eyes.

Ellis pushed past me, slathered in river mud and grinning. He threaded his fingers into the woman's tangled green hair, turned her head to get a better look.

"You got yourself a good one." Father stood behind Ellis, one hand on his son's shoulder. He was still winded from the struggle, and spoke in a slow, halting manner.

"You think I did?" said Ellis.

"Oh, yes. I can always tell."

Father remembered I'd come along, frowned when he saw the red in my eyes.

He had no patience for my sympathies.

＊

My brother called his new wife Marigold, because our late mother had told him stories of a spry yellow cat called Marigold that she'd kept as a child, and Ellis had grown to fancy that name. They tied her down to the old four poster mahogany bed that had come with my parents all the way from Virginia, back when this land still belonged to Mexico. Mr. Bolton helped my father carry in a couple of armloads of cut cedar logs, and Ellis fed them one by one into the gaping fireplace.

It was high summer, and Ellis had shuttered the windows, causing the heat to blossom and suffocate. By the time he had the fire raging, standing there in the doorway made me feel like a slab of meat in a smokehouse.

Marigold thrashed and howled as the temperature climbed. The fire threw sinister shadows up the walls and colored her agony in muted orange light.

"Takes a week or so for her to dry out?" asked Ellis.

"Give or take," said Father.

Mr. Bolton allowed that two of his wives had taken nearly a month to dry out, but the third was ready in just a few days.

"I hope she goes quicker than that," said Father. "Whole place will be hotter than Hell until she does."

We left her there alone, and Father instructed me to stay clear of that bedroom for the duration of her ordeal. But I couldn't help myself. I'd wander past from time to time, open the door just a crack and peer inside. I watched her change, little by little. It took three nights of screaming for her tailfin to dry up and rot off. Another three nights for her new legs to grow in, long and bone thin, like a newborn calf. Her slender gray teeth fell like pine needles, replaced by a woman's teeth, white as morning snow. Delicate, uncalloused hands replaced her sharp, elongated claws.

When he was younger, Ellis would pull the tails off the quick green lizards that sunned on the front porch, just to see how they'd grow back. Watching Marigold slowly break and come back together again put me in mind of that petty cruelty. I was disturbed every time Ellis did it, but I watched anyway. And I'd seek out those lizards, if they ever returned, wondering what kind of magic animated them.

What happened to the river wives was a different sort of magic, I suppose. But no less horrifying.

One Sunday afternoon we heard tentative footsteps, coming down the stairs. Ellis helped Marigold descend, his arm around her back. She wore a blue cotton night dress that belonged to Mama Agatha, and her legs trembled uncertainly beneath her.

Mama Agatha and Mama Lisbeth were clearing dust from windowsills and cobwebs from crannies, but they abandoned their rags and watched Marigold pass through the foyer like a ghost trying to catch her breath. My late mother had ordered a bit of stained glass from St. Louis for the transom over the front door, and sunlight filtered through, casting rainbows across Marigold's long blond hair. Her head darted around, surveying her new surroundings. Marigold was a beauty; her lips were red and full, and her eyes were gray whirlpools.

Their eyes were the only things that never changed.

Father was seated at the secretary desk in the corner, marking numbers into a ledger. He removed his spectacles, stood, and studied Marigold with his hands on his hips. Ellis put his palm on her cheek, turned her to face Father. They inspected Marigold like a goat ready for shearing. She was a perfect woman, carved from my brother's dreams. Father had always told us that the river women became whatever we most wanted them to be. I had no intention of ever claiming a river wife, but if I was compelled to, I feared she might become something quite unlike those ideal women conjured up by the men in our settlement.

Ellis took Marigold as his wife that very day.

There was no need for a wedding ceremony.

No God would bless their union.

*

Marigold joined the other wives in their daily tasks.

I'd follow them around as they swept the longleaf pine floors and dug potatoes from the garden. I'd sit at the kitchen table and watch as they pounded out bread dough with hands and forearms. One afternoon, I joined them in the chicken yard to gather eggs. Mama Lisbeth and Marigold went right to their business, but Mama Agatha was well into her decline, so I carried her basket and undertook her share of the work.

It wasn't a couple of years ago that Mother Agatha looked young as Mama Lisbeth, but all her teeth had rotted out and her hair was a thin silver thicket. Her deep brown skin had gone ashy gray, and every step set her trembling, like dry branches in a gale.

The sun burned away all the clouds, and the air turned wet and heavy. I walked down to the river where the ordinary women worked at the laundry, snuck a bucket of water back up to the chicken yard. The river wives ladled the water in an earthenware cup and passed it between themselves, taking slow sips with their eyes closed. I kept watch so as not to get caught.

The river wives breathed in the dank odor of the stuff with tears streaking their cheeks. For a moment, they remembered everything.

There wasn't much I could do to comfort them, but I could do this.

Mrs. Harold and her daughter Sarah walked past carrying armloads of laundry. They wore calico work dresses with the sleeves rolled up, headed for the river. Sweaty strands of hair escaped their bonnets and clung to their shoulders like river moss. They spoke in loud, happy voices, almost as if they wanted to prove to the river women that they could.

Mrs. Harold laughed at something Sarah said. The sound drew Marigold's gaze, and she made a keening noise in her throat that was easy to interpret.

Mama Lisbeth stroked Marigold's long hair, offered her another sip of the brown river water once Mrs. Harold and Sarah had disappeared into the trees. I could feel the river wives' thoughts crashing into one another like waves. I grew up imagining everyone could read what the river wives were thinking, but I learned that wasn't the case. Maybe it was my youth, and maybe it was my kindness with the water, but they trusted me, and I understood what pained them.

The river called to them like a mother's voice, but they weren't allowed to answer.

Mr. Alexander's river wife had tried to sneak down to the Brazos a few years before, deep in the middle of the night when she figured she could make it. A few of the men on the way back from an Indian patrol found her out, and she spent her last months lashed to a post at the edge of town, raising dry screams in a vain attempt to chase away the vultures.

The cup of water calmed Marigold. Her gray eyes splashed about, and her muscles relaxed. I'd noticed a bit of river water had the same effect on them as a glass of whiskey had on Ellis.

When our baskets were filled with spotted brown eggs, the women started back for the house, and Mama Agatha gripped my arm with her cold hand so I could help her along. My real mother had died during my birth, as Ellis was fond of reminding me, but Mama Agatha had assumed her role. I couldn't remember a time when Agatha wasn't there, humming tunes that put me in mind of faraway places I'd never see. Her songs were enchantments. They drew the calm from deep inside the soul, and they revealed secrets.

Mama Agatha understood things about me that I wasn't yet willing to admit to myself, but she never pushed. She allowed me to grow into myself at my own pace.

I led her along the path to the house like a child, and her frailty frightened me. River women could only exist on land for so long, and though it had been a lifetime for me, Agatha's years out of water had passed with the swiftness of a runaway stallion. I imagined I could feel her blood slowing and her heart growing still. I imagined I could smell the furious decay burrowing beneath her translucent skin.

Agatha's thoughts swam on the liquid surface of her eyes. Love for me. A bone-weary tiredness. And worst of all, a sharp desperation that I wished I could ignore. I gave thought to changing course. I could escort her the few hundred yards down to the river. The water likely wouldn't save her at this point; she was too far gone. But at the very least she might look upon the lazy flow of her river one last time, and dream of days gone by.

I knew this is what she wanted. But I still remembered the sound of Mr. Alexander's river wife, screaming from her post, and no matter how strong my love for Mama Agatha, I didn't have the nerve to free her.

Marigold and Mama Lisbeth were far ahead of us when we saw a Karankawa man watching us from the recesses of the canebrake. Not twenty feet separated us. He was lean and muscled and tattooed, wearing a deerskin breechcloth and a beaded necklace. All Father's stories about the Karankawa warned of blood and scalps, baby eating, kidnappings, and violent attacks on women.

Fear chased through me, hot and primal.

I'd only seen a live Karankawa once before. He'd been navigating a canoe up a small stream that broke off from the Brazos. Father killed him with a rifle shot from a rise overlooking the river, and the man died without ever knowing we were there. The canoe kept going, carrying his body out of sight. Father told me the man was bound for Hell anyway, and he was happy enough to help him get there faster.

I shouted for help and tried to hurry Mama Agatha away, but she used what strength she had left to plant her feet in the long grass. If I'd pulled any harder, she'd have toppled to the ground.

The Karankawa carried a wooden bow at least six feet tall, and I knew he could kill us long before we'd make it back to the house. My shouting didn't stir him. He studied Mama Agatha, taking slow steady breaths, like he was in no hurry. Men's voices filled the afternoon, answering my calls, but none of them would arrive in time.

Mama Agatha wasn't afraid. I could feel it.

She was, instead, grateful.

She locked eyes with the Karankawa, pulling at him with those gray whirlpools. She hummed one of her ancient songs. I struggled to understand the deep blue confusion of her thoughts, but finally the pure desire for death rose from the shallows.

The man released an arrow with a motion smooth as quicksilver. It struck Mama Agatha's heart, passed clean through her, and lodged into a fence post.

The Karankawa disappeared back into the canebrake and was gone before Agatha's body touched the earth.

✳

Father assembled a dozen men. They rode through the scrub brush, and along the cedar infested river bottoms, hunting the Karankawa. They appeared back at the settlement long after dark, bloody and drunk. A brace of Indian scalps hung from Father's saddle, but there was no way of knowing if one of them belonged to the man who felled Mama Agatha. Father was fond of killing Indians, blaming them for every fault and failure in the land. The Karankawa people had lived and fished along these river bottoms long before even the Mexicans arrived, but that made no difference to Father. To him, the Indians were obstacles to be cleared away, like stones from a field, so new life could grow.

I never hated *anyone* that much. Not even Father.

The hunting party congregated at our house, where the men offered condolences and drank whisky. Mama Lisbeth and Marigold served them cold dinner on the porch, and I hid away in the stifling hot kitchen, small in my grief.

The men were loud and boisterous, and I could hear most of what they said. Mr. Bolton barked that if you get seven solid years out of a river wife, you're doing better than most, and Agatha had been out of the water for near a dozen. Mr. Alexander agreed, but also believed it was a terrible shame, her making it that long, only to be killed by a god cursed savage.

Father was untouched by the tragedy, other than losing something he felt belonged to him. He'd lost interest in Agatha long ago. And besides, we all knew he'd be back down at the river again with a net soon enough.

Mama Lisbeth bled tension, and her grief hung like an added layer of heat in the kitchen. While Marigold brought more food out to the men, Lisbeth took a rest. We sat together at the table with the windows open, listening to the sounds of nightbirds and sharp, drunken laughter. We chewed hard biscuits covered in honey and shared a pitcher of buttermilk.

I fought against the intrusive, swirling nature of her thoughts. It hurt me trying to shut her out, but my misery cut deeper than hers. I'd known Agatha my whole life; she was my mother in every way but blood. And while Lisbeth mourned Agatha's death, there was something more. She wondered if Agatha's fate might not be preferable to her own. I didn't need a reminder that maybe I could have done something to save Agatha; maybe I could still do something to save Lisbeth and Marigold.

My failures and my fears were not secret to me.

I closed my eyes.

I wasn't the person to help them; I was as out of place in our world as they were.

Ellis came into the kitchen, muddy boots heavy against the floor. Lisbeth leapt into action like a startled colt.

"Why are you hiding in here?" Ellis took a seat next to me and bit into one of the biscuits. His face was sweaty and red, and I could smell the whiskey in his blood.

"I'm not hiding. Just helping."

"Helping eat all the honey and drink all the buttermilk, I guess." Ellis grinned at me, but there was something hard in his eyes that reminded me of Father. They were two of a kind. Ellis was seven years older than me, and Father had already carved him into his ideal of a man. Young and lean and strong. Eager to claim his place in the world.

Lisbeth poured him a cup of buttermilk.

Ellis put his hand on my shoulder and squeezed harder than was polite. He liked me to know how much stronger he was. He'd rinsed most of the blood from his hands and arms, but it still stained his shirt and clotted in the scruff on his cheeks.

"Real sorry about your *mother*," he said.

He always said it that way. *Mother.* Like he wanted to make it known that I'd given up all claim to our birth mother. Like caring for Agatha and Lisbeth was a weakness.

"We killed that Indian," he said.

"Looks like you killed a lot of them."

"As many as we could." Ellis patted me on the back, misunderstanding my observation for approval.

"How many?" I asked.

"Oh, I don't know for sure," he said. "But enough to keep them behaving for a while."

It snowed once when I was five, and Ellis spent all afternoon pulling me around on a sled he'd built out of spare lumber. We waged a snowball battle with the other children and climbed skinny trees slick with ice. From the boughs of one of those trees, we watched woodsmoke climb from chimneys and infiltrate the low gray clouds.

Having an older brother to share that day with had been a fine thing, indeed, but all that had changed.

"You should come out on the porch," he said. "I'll sneak you a whiskey if you want."

"I'm okay where I am."

"It's too hot to sit in here. And besides, you're getting too big to spend all your time following old women around the kitchen."

"She's not old," I said.

"Too old to be your playmate."

Lisbeth stabbed at the fire in the hearth with an iron rod. She was heating water in a pot, maybe for tea and maybe just to keep herself occupied so she could pretend not to listen. Lisbeth's auburn hair was knotted up beneath a bonnet, but gray streaks showed in the bits that escaped. Her face had grown sharper, and wrinkles pulled at her eyes. But for all that, I never thought of her as old. More *tired* I suppose. But time chased after the river women faster than it did the rest of us, and soon enough I'd be leading Lisbeth around by the arm and watching her wither down to bones just like I had with Agatha.

Ellis shook his head at me, all the while cleaning dried blood from underneath his fingernails with a knife blade. "I don't care what you do, but Father doesn't like you acting this way. You come out there and show your face for a few minutes and it'll go a long way." He gave me a questioning look like I was a wild animal with motives he couldn't predict. Maybe I'd follow him to the porch on quiet, padding feet, or maybe I'd bite.

I wasn't sure about myself anymore either.

I only knew that being around Father and the other men made me intensely uncomfortable. They expected so many things from me that couldn't be reconciled with my own desires.

Father told me time and again how the men in this world must take what they want, else they'd wind up with nothing but leftovers and regrets. When he'd moved the family here from Virginia, he hadn't bothered with Mr. Austin and the old impresario's land grants. Father encamped farther downriver, in open defiance of Mexican law, and claimed a league of rich, black soil bottomland for himself. When the revolution happened, he marched off with a musket and came back a citizen of the Republic of Texas, with all the rights of a free landowner.

This was *his* small patch of earth now, and he never lost one night of sleep worrying about how he got it.

I wanted no part of it. I didn't want to inherit his farm, and though I was still quite young, I already knew I had no interest in taking a river wife. No interest in taking *any* wife, to tell it true. Maybe that's what Father saw in me that made him hate me so much.

But what I wanted didn't matter. Time would chase me down soon enough, just like it did the river women. The prospect of growing up terrified me.

Ellis waited for me to submit, but the silence dragged on like a song we were all tired of singing.

"You've been wrong since you were born," said Ellis.

"I guess maybe I have been."

Ellis hated when I didn't react to his meanness. I figured he'd box my ears like usual, but he acted like he didn't hear me.

"Maybe if you hadn't killed our mother, you'd have more than these animals to raise you up right."

Lisbeth hissed. Her anger was a sudden spike to my brain. Ellis pushed back the chair and the legs scraped against the floor with a sound like a sawblade cutting timber.

"You will tend to your own business, Lisbeth," he said. "You hear me?"

Lisbeth couldn't respond, but she turned away from us with a flush of fear that was hot against my skin.

Ellis stood over me, hair wild and tangled. He was unsteady on his feet, and I wondered for a second if I could tackle him. Things might have escalated then and there if Marigold hadn't walked into the kitchen with an empty serving tray and stopped in her tracks, unable to stifle a sharp gasp at the unexpected presence of her husband. Ellis took the tray from her and tossed it on the table. He put an arm around her shoulders and drew her in close.

Marigold went slack at his touch, and the dull resignation she projected made the milk sit heavy in my stomach.

"You may do as you wish," Ellis said to me. "But I will take everything I've earned, and I won't apologize for it."

Ellis was talking, but the words belonged to Father.

He left then, sweeping Marigold along, and Lisbeth sat back down across from me. She made a mewling sound that was as close as she ever came to crying. I took her hands and held them. We sat together, listening until the revels died down.

And we stayed that way until daylight came rushing over the horizon.

*

A week later, Marigold drank too much river water.

Father and Ellis were off chasing milk cows and half wild mustangs. I spent the morning following Marigold and Lisbeth around, helping with their chores, and by early afternoon we found ourselves in the orchard, gathering peaches and pears and figs in woven baskets.

The river was close. I could hear it cutting a path toward the ocean. I could smell the lake weeds and the fish. Sunlight splashed off the water and sparkled through the trees. Only the fear of being captured kept Marigold and Lisbeth from going home.

Chances are they'd make it. But what if they didn't?

They grew melancholy, being so close. Giving them river water like I did might have made it worse, but it was a forbidden kindness I couldn't resist.

I'd fetched a full bucket while they were plucking fruit from the trees, and now it was nearly empty. Mama Lisbeth had taken only one cupful, but Marigold had indulged with a destructive fervor. Insects hummed from the shadows, and Marigold swayed like she was dancing to their strange music. I had never seen her this way. Her liquid eyes raged like storm-tossed seas and her cheeks flushed red as new scales rippled beneath her human skin.

All of this from a half bucket of water. I wondered how quickly Marigold would regain herself if she waded into the river.

Her thoughts lashed out, slapped me like horsewhips.

She kept no secrets hidden.

Marigold spun with her arms out, her golden hair on the wind, and she showed me memories of rushing water and winding underground rivers so deep that sunlight never found them. She might live a thousand years in the cold depths of the sea, but every breath on land brought her closer to the end. Her bare feet crashed against hard soil as she danced; her legs were abominations. There was no grace in her motion. She spun like a tornado, like she hoped to draw all the sharp and broken things close to her and send them flying outward again, tearing apart everything men had built here. Lisbeth grew frightened, looked around to make sure no one had spotted the commotion. She grabbed Marigold and pulled her down to the ground. Marigold screeched, but Lisbeth held her tight. Marigold struggled, finally shoved Lisbeth away, and she crawled toward me shedding alabaster skin and old secrets.

Marigold's eyes were waterfalls, pouring from their sockets, and I couldn't look away.

Memories flowed from Agatha to Lisbeth to Marigold to me. The river might keep secrets from the land, but never from those who belong to her.

Marigold showed me a woman floating down the Brazos, face up with her hair fanned out along the brown surface, dead eyes clotted with cypress leaves.

She showed me the face of my mother.

And yet, it wasn't my true mother. That much I understood. This was not a woman who'd died in childbirth. This was a woman enraged. Horrified and *embarrassed* that one of the creatures her husband cultivated had given him a son, just as she had. The babe could never be a brother to Ellis. She'd taken the crying child, the *unnatural* child, and swaddled it in dishtowels, secreted it away while her husband followed oxen through the field, while her young son chased frogs and lizards, while the river women worked the butter churn.

She had taken the babe to the river.

She had taken *me* there.

And it had not gone well for her.

We were drunk on memories, not keeping a watch. The men found us there on our knees in the orchard, and we never heard them coming. Marigold howled, lurched upward. Ellis had grabbed her hair and pulled her to her feet. She hissed. A few of her sharp bits had returned. Stray teeth, one long razored thumbnail. A ridge of copper scales began at her nose and traced down both cheekbones. The skin on her neck had come loose and it flapped like laundry on the line.

Father came up behind Ellis, saw Marigold covered in gray blood and fighting to regain herself. Father's face twisted up like he'd tasted something awful. Ellis backed away, afraid of his lovely young wife.

Couldn't they see Marigold had become more interesting and more beautiful than she'd ever been before?

Father saw the overturned bucket, figured out exactly what was happening. "Ellis, take your woman to the house so we can dry her out again."

Ellis had lost the color from his face. He looked younger than his seventeen years. "I don't think . . ."

"Take your woman to the goddamn house!"

Ellis was more afraid of Father than he was Marigold.

He advanced on her, tried to take her arm and pull her along like he always did. Marigold let him bring her close, then she tore out his throat with her teeth.

Father struck Marigold hard enough to knock her to her knees again. Ellis fell, air whistling from the empty place where his throat had been. Marigold tried to stand, and Father hit her again. Something in her jaw broke loose and slid sideways. I climbed Father's back, trying to pull him away. He shook me loose, put me on the ground and kicked me in the ribs. One of them snapped with a sound like a tree branch breaking in a storm, and it stabbed into me with every breath.

Father loomed over me. "Should have tied you up in a grain sack when you were born and tossed you in the river."

He kicked me again, snapped one of my fingers when I tried to grab his boot to stop him.

I'm confident he'd have killed me if Mama Lisbeth hadn't taken the woven basket, heavy with pears, and hammered it against the back of his head. The blow wasn't near enough to kill him, but it was enough to topple him to the ground and momentarily steal his wits. It was enough to buy us a few seconds.

No option remained except to run.

I helped Marigold to her feet, and together we followed Mama Lisbeth past the canebrake and into the tight web of cedars that stretched from the settlement down to the river. Branches slashed and blood flowed. Marigold's fury was a living thing, casting out in all directions like a fisherman's line, catching everyone it could. She was not her true self again, not yet, but the water was empowering, and no river woman in the settlement failed to understand her pleading, her urgent command. *This* was the time; *this* was the opportunity. Everyone at once. Coordinated escape. I could hear the rasp of kitchen knives against bare throats, and the clatter of spoons against fine china as they stirred poison into black coffee. I could hear hammers collapsing skulls and powerful men screaming as they were shoved bodily into blazing hearths. Marigold shared her rage with the river, and the river shared it with us all.

We reached the water and Marigold didn't slow. She splashed through the shallows until the water was deep enough to swim. Flesh peeled away and carried downriver in a torrent of blood. Her tail tore through the remains of her human body and slapped the water.

Marigold dove beneath and was gone.

Lisbeth waded into the river with more hesitancy, as if long years of conditioning assured her this could not possibly be happening. Knee deep in the water, she smiled as the skin on her legs split up the sides like fabric coming apart at the seams. She waved for me to follow, then swam out to deeper waters.

She called out to me. The *river* called out to me.

But how was I supposed to follow?

I'd swam here a hundred times, and the water didn't affect me. Still, the river whispered and begged, assured me there was no better life than sleeping in sunken temples and navigating barnacled shipwrecks spun with seaweed. Mama Agatha was my birth mother—I understood that now—and I belonged to the river. The river had saved me from being murdered as a babe. Had risen and drowned my father's wife or summoned *something cold* to pry me from her hands and send her corpse floating away into oblivion.

I was a child of the river, and I belonged here.

Either that, or the river was lying.

My eyes burned and every breath was agony. No home remained for me on land, but I was too afraid to seek a home in the water. And Father could not be far behind.

Then I heard one of the songs Mama Agatha used to sing to me. A cradle song, old as the sea itself.

Mama Lisbeth was singing me home.

I waded out up to my waist, still uncertain, until I saw children pour from the trees and splash into the water. Sarah Harold and her brother Seth. Amos and Louisa and the Noble twins, barely old enough to walk down to the river on their own. A dozen more at least. All of them, laughing and singing along. Mama Lisbeth called out, and they came. Her song grew louder, and the children walked toward her, not bothering to swim when the water got deep, but pressing on as if their shoes were filled with lead and they could not float. Heads sank beneath the muddy flow, and the children disappeared, one by one.

The song summoned me too, and I walked until the water lapped at my chin. Mama Lisbeth watched me approach, way out in the middle of the river now. Her voice cut through my bones, gave me no choice but to wade deeper, to join the children's chorus.

Lisbeth's gray eyes drew me in and the sunlight against her scales was blinding. Her smile was sharp, and her soul was vengeance.

Did all these children belong to the river?

I didn't hold my breath and I didn't cry.

I let the Brazos swallow me up and take me home.

LOVE KILLS

The first time my mother killed me I was seven.

She told me it wouldn't hurt. Even at that age I knew she was lying, but she was my mother and I wanted to make her happy.

I didn't strain against the clothesline that bound my wrists and ankles to the kitchen table. When she drew the knife across my throat, the cold was a living thing, blooming in my chest and escaping my mouth in a wet gasp. My mother let the blood collect in the same yellow plastic bowl she'd used to mix the batter for my birthday cake just a few weeks earlier. All the while she whispered how much she loved me.

Mama chanted her words. The sigil she'd painted on my chest burned. I didn't understand yet that hers was a desperate sort of magic. The magic of easy answers.

The magic of getting by.

She was my mother and she needed me to die.

So, I did.

✶

The second time my mother killed me, I fought back.

I arrived home from middle school and found Mama on the couch, working her way through a pack of Winston Lights like it was her job. The thin living room curtains were drawn, and the television glow cast a smoky blue haze across her face.

"Come sit for a minute, honey." She had a half empty bottle of grocery store wine in one hand, and a revolver in the other.

The recliner groaned when I sat, and bits of stuffing poked free from a tear along the padded armrest.

The motion of sitting burned my muscles and caused a popping sound in my bones. My spine was shaped like a fishhook, my back muscles elongated.

You can't expect to die and come back unchanged.

Mama shook her head, like she was trying to deny her own instinct. "I'm sorry, but I've got to try this again."

"Why do you have to try it with me?"

"It has to be somebody I love. Otherwise, it's not a sacrifice. Who else do I have?"

The spell hadn't worked quite right the first time. The sacrifice hadn't led to wealth or romance or happiness.

The killing hadn't *taken*.

Mama languished on the couch in her terry cloth bathrobe and house shoes with the soles peeling away.

"I think I have the right spell this time."

"I don't want to die."

Mama whispered some words under her breath. She stood, the gun heavy in her hand. "Please remember how much I love you. Else you know this wouldn't work."

I pushed up from the chair, lunged for her. I got hold of her wrist, tried to shake the gun loose, but she hammered me with the wine bottle and that put me down.

One gunshot to my chest followed, and she dipped her fingers into the meat of my heart and used it to trace symbols on the walls.

"Thank you, honey."

My blood burned against the walls with a fierce golden light.

I remained on my back, watching the brown water stains on the ceiling. Then I died. Again.

∗

The third time my mother killed me, I helped her.

If I had been able to remain in school, I might have been graduating then, but instead I crouched on the edge of my bed as Mama unbolted the locks on my door, one by one, and came in with a spell book and a butcher knife.

"You sure you're ready" she asked.

"Yeah, I'm sure."

She approached and I sat forward, rearranging my twisted muscles and misplaced bones into the most human shape I could summon.

My hair fell long and matted; I'd chewed my unclipped fingernails into points.

Mama put the tip of the knife against my breastbone.

"You'll get it right this time?" I asked.

"Yes. I'm so sorry. This time it won't go wrong."

"I hope you finally get whatever it is you need."

"I just haven't been happy for so long."

"I know."

I put my hands around hers, felt the blood run hot beneath her skin. Together we gripped the knife. I pulled it toward me, felt the bite.

Prayed that this would be the last time.

✱

The fourth time my mother killed me, I begged her to.

I prowled on all fours, blood hungry. Most of my humanity left behind in the grave.

"Please." My voice was a rumble at the back of my throat.

"I want to make sure I don't screw up!" Mama dug through a pile of old spell books, fingers running against yellow pages. Artifacts cluttered the tabletop—amulets, daggers, a tarnished brass bell. "Just give me time."

"No time." I stalked closer, smelling her copper stench. Smelling the wet paper and the mold of ages. The sound of her thundering heart drew me to her in a thirsty rush.

She defended herself with a ceremonial sword. Halved my body with the first blow. Took off my head with the second.

"Mama," I whispered. "Please."

Mama lifted the blade, eyes wild and wet with tears, then she finished the job.

✱

The last time my mother killed me, she killed us both.

I rattled the bars of my cage as she dumped a whole can of gasoline around the living room and struck a match.

"I can't do this to either of us anymore," she said.

I howled, trying to voice my misery. I was a monster who couldn't die. My own nature had corrupted my mother's spells. I wouldn't consider the only other reason we might have come to this point. That my mother never *really* loved me. That I wasn't a suitable sacrifice, no matter how fervently she'd tried to convince herself that I was.

"I love you," she lied. "I really do."

Then she dropped the match, and the fire told the truth.

CONSTELLATION BURN

Jordan was on the run again.

No fixed direction, just a fast escape from her life with Tad, and a hitched ride with a talkative long-haul driver on his way to El Paso. The driver pulled into a truck stop, bought her a charred hamburger and some black coffee, then left her to haunt the diesel pumps, a lost soul gone ghost white beneath the glow of industrial halides. Jordan sat on a duffel bag stuffed with everything she'd had time to pack. The earth beneath her shuddered every time a rig moved past on the interstate and blood accelerated in her veins with the adrenaline of what she'd done. She might have lingered there forever, letting the wind chew her away, but she noticed a pickup truck idling in front of her, the passenger door thrown open, and a man inside, offering a ride.

"I can keep you safe," he said.

Jordan's head pounded. Her last cigarette hung from her lips, burned nearly to the filter. The man's words assumed things about her situation. He was good-looking, maybe five, ten years older than Jordan, a big man with work muscles and a mustache clipped short. A cowboy hat shaded half his face, but the dash lights still picked out his grin. He patted the seat in a manner he must have thought reassuring.

Jordan understood whatever the man was offering might not be better than what she was running from, but he didn't ask her about the cooling yellow bruises on her arms, or the livid blue marks around her neck. The pickup engine idled and air brakes hissed from the diesel yard, but the man kept quiet, giving her the space to consider her diminishing options. Tad with his meth black teeth. The way his rough hands moved along her body and the blossoming pain. Jordan lived at the bottom of a grave, and if she didn't keep moving, someone would shovel dirt on top of her.

"There are places in the world you can hide," the man said. "Places nobody will ever find you, no matter how hard they look."

Jordan took the last drag from her cigarette, tossed it into the gravel along the road. She hefted her duffel into the truck bed and climbed into the passenger seat.

The man's name was Altus. His truck cabin smelled like oily rags and summer sweat, and the air conditioner chugged out thin granules of sand. Altus directed the truck onto the interstate, and a few miles later, turned off onto one of the farm roads. Darkness dropped around them, and the universe constricted. Not for the first time, Jordan felt herself being absorbed into someone else's reality, and she realized a threshold had been crossed, some cosmic force had set her in motion, and she was just along for the ride. Already she was reconsidering her decision to climb into the stranger's truck, but when he spoke, it was in a slow, kind drawl, and he had an easy laugh. When he put his hand on her knee, she let it stay there.

For better or worse.

*

Altus had seven daughters. Each of them beautiful, and each of them so alike that Jordan had trouble telling one from another. Their bright eyes watched the truck arrive, and their delicate hands opened the passenger door, hefted Jordan's duffel, grasped at her wrists and forearms and helped ease her from the cab like precious cargo. Seven mouths moved, lips whispering *mother, mother, mother*, and Jordan felt the ground shifting beneath her tennis shoes as the world urged her back into motion.

You might want to keep running, Jordan.

Altus had told her the truth. He carried Jordan somewhere nobody would ever find her. She stood surrounded by strangers in a caliche parking lot with nothing but the vast expanse of night in every direction. A low building ran the length of the property, some hybrid of a filling station, a convenience store, and a bar, all bathed in the dingy yellow light of an overhead sign that read ROUGHNECK ROOST. Outbuildings crowded in the near distance, Altus's house and a pair of storage sheds. Beyond the compound's dim perimeter, nothing was visible save for the lights of a few faraway drilling rigs, each of them flickering like cold constellations in the blackness of space.

Altus led Jordan around the bar and toward the house, a squat box with green aluminum siding and a metal roof. He steered her with one hand on the small of her back. His daughters followed, continuing to whisper *mother, mother, mother* until they reached the front door and Altus turned to position himself between Jordan and the hovering young women. The lights played tricks on Jordan's eyes. The women looked wispy at the edges, like someone was pulling at their threads, unravelling their being.

"She's not your mother."

She most certainly wasn't. The women appeared to be in their mid-twenties, nearly as old as Jordan. Altus wasn't old enough to have children that age. But he introduced them as his daughters, naming them one by one in dizzying succession—*Dauphine, Elspeth, Polly, Marisol, Pith, Sumner, and Fetch.* They curtsied one after another, bowing their heads at the same precise angle, carbon copy beauties in yellow sundresses and cowboy boots. After this presentation, Altus suggested they be about their chores, and as a unit the women backed away, eyes still on Jordan as if she might disappear into memory if they lost sight of her.

Altus took hold of Jordan's arm, pulled her inside the house, and turned the deadbolt.

They shared Altus's bed, the sheets musty and knotted. Tattoos covered Altus's chest, spirals and broken triangles and shapes of questionable geometry. The tattoos blurred in the blue darkness when Jordan tried to study them, and they eluded every attempt to trace them with her fingertips. An oscillating fan hummed, pushed heat around the bedroom. Jordan lay there with her heart hammering. This might be a worse situation than the one she'd fled.

Animals moved on the roof, claws clattering against metal. Something heavy shifted overhead. In Jordan's mind, it was the seven sisters, clambering up the walls and sniffing around the eaves. Pressing themselves up against the roof, listening to her breathe and trying to read her thoughts. It was a crazy notion, but there was something off about the way the women moved and the intense way they watched her. Altus rolled on his side and stared at her, so close she could feel the heat of his breath. The sliver of a smile on his face confirmed every wild scenario she could conjure.

"Don't let them girls get to you," he said. "They like to mess around in your head. That's their nature. But they belong to me. I won't let them harm you."

"They're all your daughters?"

"That's what I told you."

That wasn't exactly an answer, so Jordan persisted.

"Where's their mother at?"

"There's no mother could birth them girls."

Jordan didn't know what to make of that. Was he saying their mother had died in childbirth, or that they'd come to him by other means? Maybe Altus liked collecting strays. If that was the case, Jordan might be just another addition to his coterie.

But no, she didn't believe that. Jordan might be a runaway from life, short on options, but those others were something else entirely. She didn't have much choice but to endure the night, but Jordan decided the next morning she'd hitch back to the interstate.

As it happened, she stayed with Altus and his daughters for nearly a month.

✳

Altus gave Jordan a job in the convenience store that was attached to the filling station—or more accurately, he installed her there behind the counter to pay for the food she ate and the roof she slept under. Altus hadn't offered a paycheck, but Jordan figured this wasn't a bad way to spin her wheels until she could figure out what direction she was headed. Altus kept her supplied with Winston Lights and Lone Star, and he was a softer touch than Tad. She was aware he'd caught her in a sort of trap, but she felt her chances of escape were good if she ever made up her mind to leave.

The mystery of his daughters is what *really* trapped her. No matter how hard Jordan tried to get a read on them, their story was written in a language she couldn't understand.

The store had floor-to-ceiling windows that faced the endless flatlands of the West Texas oil patch. Jordan counted one day after another, surrounded by racks of candy bars and potato chips, yellow pints of motor oil and road maps collecting dust. Fried burritos and corn dogs grew stale beneath an orange heat lamp, covering everything in a constant layer of grease. Jordan read the tabloids, trying to ignore the cloying smell. On the hottest days, she'd stand at the Dr. Pepper cooler with the door open, breathe in the frosted air. Out beyond the gas pumps, the sun stormed against the earth. It was enough to discourage any idle notions of setting off on foot. Jordan scratched lottery tickets with a quarter, happy to be indoors.

Out there, the real world lurked in all its fury.

The customers were mostly highway patrolmen who stopped in for gas and chewing gum, or truckloads of rowdy men who worked the rigs. They arrived when the shifts changed, so regular you could set your watch. Roughnecks with steel-toed boots and filthy coveralls, hardhats left behind on the dashboards of oil field pickups. The same men who'd wander next door to the bar in the evenings for burgers, chicken wings, and shots of mezcal.

One afternoon, a regular named Hobie walked in, fresh off the rig and smelling like it. Every day was the same—a Miller Lite tallboy from the ice chest to down on his way over to the bar, and a packet of Red Man chew. Jordan figured he chose Red Man because she had to turn behind the counter and reach up high to get it off the shelf, giving him a nice long look at her ass. Hobie was the sort who let his eyes linger too long. Jordan had known plenty like him.

She placed the chewing tobacco on the counter next to his beer, watched as he pulled a wadded twenty-dollar bill from his pocket and straightened it.

"Thank you, darling," he said.

"You need anything else?"

"There's a whole lot I need, if you're offering."

"I'm not."

"That's a shame," he said. "Awful lot of you I want."

"Altus is liable to beat you with a lug wrench if he finds out you're hitting on me."

"Well, you ain't going to tell him nothing." Hobie smiled, stretching his homely face tight against his skull. Hobie was probably forty-five, but he looked sixty. Skin furrowed and red, enough hair left on his head to pretend he wasn't an old man. When Jordan rang him up and passed his change back, he made sure to touch her fingers.

"I'm serious," he said. "Rented me a house over in Pecos. Real nice. You come live with me you won't be working in no filling station. I'll take care of you."

"How come everyone thinks I need taking care of?"

"I'm just offering."

Jordan's bones would grow restless again, but when she left this place, she promised herself it wouldn't be to follow a man like Hobie.

The bell over the door rang, and one of Altus's daughters moved into the store.

It was still hard for Jordan to tell them apart, but she was pretty sure it was Fetch. The woman sat down on the aluminum bar stool near the window, placed there for anyone who preferred to dine-in on their shitty gas station food. She waved, showing the tattoos running up her forearm. Same ones Altus had. Same ones they all had. The air around her looked like one of the heat waves that crawled along the blacktop, and Jordan felt the lightheaded sensation she'd come to associate with one of Altus's daughters exerting her will.

Fetch crossed her ankles, stared at Hobie like she was studying him for a test.

Hobie forgot about Jordan straight away.

He locked in on Fetch, the color emptying from his face. Jordan had been on the receiving end of the kind of attention Fetch was giving him. Altus's daughters had a way of burrowing inside your brain and picking at the things you wanted kept secret. Hobie stood still, barely breathing, and Jordan felt the air constrict as Fetch pulled out Hobie's fears and showed them to him. Stray thoughts buzzed around like houseflies over a trashcan, and Jordan couldn't help but catch a few of them.

Two months behind on that rent house. Bank calling about his pickup. A persistent pain in his left lung that he didn't want to tell anyone about. A pure, adrenalized terror about what life was going to be like for him in five years. In ten. Working on a rig was fine when he was fresh out of high school, but fast forward thirty years and the finish line was coming like a freight train. What happens when his body breaks down and the only way he's ever known to earn a living isn't an option anymore? Pain chased through his back and his legs and worse, his hands, and there were a dozen new guys every year without the wear of age to slow them down.

Tears welled in Hobie's red eyes.

When Fetch finally relented, Hobie grabbed his beer and tobacco from the counter, escaped out the front door like the devil was at his heels.

Fetch turned her eyes to Jordan and whispered the only thing she'd ever heard any of the daughters say—*mother, mother, mother.*

Jordan offered her the best smile she could muster, and Fetch smiled back, the corners of her mouth stretched out far too wide for a normal face.

This might have scared Jordan when she first arrived, but she knew Fetch didn't have a problem with her.

The daughters had already mined Jordan's secrets. They knew about what she'd done to Tad. Or at least what she was pretty sure she'd done. And they knew a whole lot more, besides. None of it seemed to matter to them, and as far as Jordan knew, they hadn't said anything about it to Altus.

For that, Jordan was grateful.

✳

Jordan had trouble sleeping, and oftentimes she'd head outside in the middle of the night to sit in one of the aluminum folding chairs that Altus kept by his oil drum barbeque smoker. The seven daughters would break apart from the shadows and join her. They'd perch awkwardly in one of the chairs or drop to the ground and sit cross-legged in the sticker burrs. Night air burned hot against Jordan's skin, and she'd light a cigarette to chase away the sulfurous smell of the oil fields. She wondered where the daughters went at night, when she wasn't around. They never came in the house. Jordan had asked Altus, and he said they did whatever the hell it was they wanted to do. According to him, he could manage them easier during the day, but in the deep darkness they were powerful. And they followed their own wills. Altus had given up trying to tame them.

Night held them all in sway. The daughters would stare into the black, seeking out something in the impossible distance or lost in their own thoughts. Jordan could never tell. She didn't mind; she appreciated the silence. They weren't there to ask anything of her. They had no advice to offer, or criticisms to level about the way she'd lived her life. And despite the fact one of them would occasionally whisper—*mother, mother, mother*—it seemed to Jordan they were looking after her, not the other way around. They seemed territorial when it came to Jordan, even deferring to her ahead of Altus sometimes, which rubbed him raw.

She had no idea how to solve the mystery of these women, but in the long hours before dawn, she was content to let them keep their secrets.

✱

Altus was always up early, said he liked to watch the stars die. Sometimes Jordan would find him standing along the highway, naked with his arms in the air. Those tattoos moved along his body, never staying put. In the night sky, constellations crashed and spun in swirls of purple and green. They'd flare red and gold, like the stars were exploding a billion years ago. Altus moved his hands like a conductor, making like he was the one moving everything around. He'd howl at the sky and claim it was a sort of prayer. Sometimes his daughters would stand rigid and stare at the spectacle overhead. Other times they'd hide out until the sun came up. Altus's ritual, if that's what it was, always gave Jordan a queasy, drunk sort of feeling.

She wasn't used to so much wide-open space. Jordan was born in Houston where you couldn't see many stars, and the ones you could stayed put.

When the last traces of night ebbed, Altus would fall to his knees in the dirt. One morning, Jordan sat down there beside him, watched his chest heave as he tried to slow his breathing. Sweat sheened his skin and he had a wild look in his eyes, like his sanity was a slowly dimming lightbulb.

"This is a strange place." Jordan sipped some instant coffee, leaving the cup against her lip for a second so she could take in the smell and the warmth.

Altus shook his head, like he was denying her assertion. "You'll be safe here, Jordan. Nothing bad's going to happen to you."

"I wasn't expecting it to."

"Just saying you're okay here."

"You know I don't plan to stay forever?"

Altus kept on shaking his head. "Where the hell would you go? Out there, the world is a noose getting pulled tight around your neck. Here in this place, you can breathe. I already told you, nobody can find you."

"Nobody's looking for me."

"You sure about that?"

And Jordan understood.

All the things Altus's daughters had plucked from her mind, they'd shared with him.

Jordan's dad, swinging from his neck in the garage while his little girl watched. The hate that boiled between Jordan and her mother. Like she thought it was Jordan's fault her husband decided being dead was better than staying in their marriage. The way Jordan snuck out of her home at seventeen and kept running from place to place with nowhere safe to light for long, until her older brother found her, beat her nearly half to death trying to get her to come home. But she kept on running. A blur of shitty jobs and half-ass boyfriends that culminated in Tad's hands around her throat, squeezing her life away, and Jordan reaching into her pocket, pulling out the one-handed flip knife her Dad had given her to protect herself. And that knife, going deep into the side of Tad's neck.

Jordan wasn't sure whether she'd killed him. But he'd been still on the bedroom floor when she left, and there had been so much blood.

"Them girls belong to me. We ain't got no secrets."

Jordan knew that much wasn't true. Fetch hadn't told him anything about Hobie and his advances, for one thing.

Still, she couldn't help but feel a little betrayed.

"Nobody *belongs* to you. You talk about them like they're your pets or something."

"Might as well be."

"What an asshole you are."

Jordan tried to stand, but Altus grabbed her forearm, pulled her back to the ground beside him. She'd finished her coffee, or she might have thrown the remains in his face. Her head was still spinning from the lightshow with the stars, and her heart was a runaway train in her chest.

"Sit your ass down and I'll explain."

"Let me go."

He released her arm, but she knew if she tried to leave again, he'd pull her back down. Altus wasn't the first man who thought he knew what was best for her. Not the first one who'd started going hard when she made it known she could figure that out for herself.

"The girls, they're my fallen stars."

"Listen to yourself, Altus."

"Came down like rockets when they fell. Maybe they're angels. I don't know. But something up there sent them here."

"There's nobody up in the sky looking after this shitty patch of dirt," Jordan said.

"You're wrong about that."

"Why would anyone care that much about this place?"

"I don't know for sure. I'm thinking it's not the place so much as the people. I was feeling empty inside, needed something to fill me up, and down they came from the sky. I love every one of them."

"Seven sweet little angels sent to wait on you hand and foot? And me number eight, I guess."

It was all so boring to Jordan. Another guy who figured he was the center of the universe. There was something about his *daughters* that was supernatural, if that's what you wanted to call it, but that didn't mean they'd been sent here to serve him.

"Just keep pissing for a fight," he said. "You're liable to get what you want."

Jordan stood, dusted off her pants. "I got to open the store. I don't have time for this."

"I ain't stopping you."

She left him sitting alongside the road, eyes closed. Soaking up the sunlight beginning to blaze up over the oil fields.

Crazy motherfucker.

Or, at least, Jordan hoped he was.

*

The rig workers passed through the convenience store that morning like unquiet spirits, bleary and near silent, like the repetition of their lives had unmoored them from reality in some way. Jordan understood. She rang up their energy drinks, beef jerky, and breakfast tacos wrapped in aluminum foil. She chain-smoked and took their money with resigned thank yous. When the rush slowed, she slapped greasy playing cards down against the countertop. Her games of solitaire always seemed to come up a card or two short.

Elspeth came into the store that afternoon, stood at the counter and watched Jordan shuffle the cards. The beer cooler hummed. Desert wind boomed against the front windowpanes. Elspeth stood quiet, stone still, not even breathing. She watched Jordan play for a good half-hour, serious and attentive, like every flip of the cards meant life or death.

When she finally spoke, she didn't say *mother*. And the voice coming from her mouth belonged to someone else.

"You're the prettiest little girl I ever seen," said Elspeth. "And smart as a whip. I love you more than anything, Jordan. Long as I'm around, you'll always have someone to look after you. And I ain't going nowhere."

Jordan put down the playing cards. Blood pounded hot inside her head, and her breath caught in her throat. It was Elspeth in front of her, eyes still set on the seven of clubs, but her voice was a perfect mimic of Jordan's dad.

"What are you doing?" asked Jordan.

Elspeth's spoke again, and this time it was Jordan's mother's voice coming from her mouth. "None of what happened was your fault, honey. Sometimes life is hard, and things don't work out. Ain't nothing to do about it but pick up and go on. Try to find some better way to be. You keep doing that. Ain't no doubt in my mind you're meant for something better than what you started with. There's always been something special about you."

Elspeth didn't look at Jordan, just kept talking, and her voice shifted, became Baker's voice. Jordan's brother.

"Listen, Jordan. I'm sorry. I'm an asshole, okay? No big revelation there. Go live your life however you want. Love you, little sister."

"Please stop talking," said Jordan.

Elspeth looked up from the cards, finally met Jordan's stare. Her lips moved, and Tad's voice emerged.

"Don't worry about me. It'll only drag you down. Everybody knows I needed killing. Ain't no crime to give a man like that what he deserves."

Jordan's eyes flushed with tears. She recognized the voices, but not what they were saying.

None of this was real.

Elspeth meant this as a kindness. Jordan knew that much. But the sound of those voices, saying things they'd never have said in a million years, stirred up a storm of dread inside her.

"Elspeth. Please go."

"If you didn't kill me, I'd have killed you."

Still Tad's voice.

"Elspeth." Jordan spoke in a whisper.

Elspeth backed away, hovered near the exit.

"This is when you really start living," she said, in a voice Jordan mercifully could not recognize. Elspeth's own voice, sounding out without reservation for the first time. "This is the beginning of everything."

When Elspeth left, Jordan pulled a bottle of Shiner from the cooler, drank it down in one shot.

Followed that one with a couple more.

✱

Jordan wandered next door to the bar when she closed the store. She joined Altus in the back-corner booth that he occupied most nights. The Formica tabletop was already wet with drink sweat, and a half-dozen empty shot glasses stood upside down in a row, like overturned tombstones. Altus tore the cellophane off a new pack of cigarettes, grinned at Jordan.

"Back for more?"

"I'm not in the mood to fight," said Jordan.

Altus was breathing heavy and already sweating alcohol. He chewed at his thumbnail. Obviously still bent out of shape from that morning and wanting to make his displeasure known. "We ain't fighting. We're *discussing*."

Polly came out from behind the bar, placed a vodka tonic and a cocktail napkin in front of Jordan. Left another shot of tequila and a Lone Star chaser for Altus. Her face stretched into one of those too-wide smiles and then she was gone to another table.

All of Altus's daughters worked in the bar—mixing drinks, wiping down tables, working the deep fryer—none of them ever saying a word.

Just *knowing* what every customer wanted before they asked. Something in their nature compelled the patrons to accept this strangeness while they were in its grip. Neon red smoke, cramped booths with torn vinyl and broken springs, the kind of old-style country music Jordan's dad used to like, lingering in the background like it had been there forever and would be there long after everyone was dead. All those tired, aching men thinking they'd have a shot at taking home one of the girls, but of course that was never going to happen. They'd pay their money, drink themselves into delirium, and the seven daughters would have the last stragglers booted to the parking lot before the clock struck five after two.

Next night, they'd do it all again.

"My girls are a sight, ain't they?" Altus threw back the shot, slammed the glass down.

"Your daughters, you mean."

"Yeah, my daughters then."

"You let your *daughters* get treated like that?"

Jordan pointed at Hobie, who was seated at the bar. He put his hand on Marisol's ass every time she walked past.

"Hobie's alright," said Altus.

"He's an asshole."

"Might be. But in my experience, that sort usually gets what's coming to them. She's liable to slap him."

Something Elspeth said crawled through Jordan's mind. *Ain't no crime to give a man like that what he deserves.*

"*That sort*, huh."

Altus took a swig of beer, pointed the mouth of the bottle at Jordan when he spoke. "I ain't never been nothing but sweet to you. Don't try to say otherwise. I told you I'd keep you safe, and I hid you out here in the safest place there is. I brought you here and gave you a family."

"We're a family then?"

Polly delivered another shot and Altus sipped it this time. "For now, at least. We play the parts they expect us to. I'm the father, you're the mother."

"I'm not anybody's mother."

"Maybe, maybe not."

"Quit pretending like you have any idea why they're here. You're just as lost as me."

"Why don't you fuck off, Jordan?"

"I'll get right on that," she said. "Just let me finish my drink first."

Altus grabbed the back of her neck, squeezed hard. Jordan jerked loose, but he grabbed her again and forced her to look at him.

"You're a real bitch tonight, ain't you?"

Altus's eyes took on a brittle, glassy look, one Jordan had seen in men's eyes too many times. Like the civilized part of his nature had been caged up, and the animal left free to hunt. Jordan wondered if he might try to hit her, but she stared at him in silence until the weight of his own intentions bore down. Half the bar watched them while pretending to sip at their drinks, and all seven daughters gathered together, joined their voices—*mother, mother, mother*—until finally Altus let go of Jordan, finished off his shot and signaled for another.

Altus exhaled through his teeth. "You ain't as smart as you think, Jordan. You're only here because they wanted you here. I didn't find you by accident."

Jordan drank her anger into a corner, found a warm, safe place inside herself to avoid any more of Altus's paranoid bullshit. Maybe something had lured her here for a reason, but that didn't mean she had to give up and go with the flow. Altus was rooted in this spot, willing to let himself be maneuvered like a game piece on a playing board. But Jordan was a mover. She could quit this place whenever she wanted, whether she'd finished playing her part in the game or not.

But her destructive side wanted to see it through.

The night wore on to the edge of closing time, until it was just Hobie left, warming a bottle of beer in his hands, eyes cruising the room in pursuit of the daughters as they wiped down tabletops and stacked chairs. Marisol came up beside him to gather his empties from the bar, put them on a tray. Hobie said something to her, but the jukebox was cranking out Faron Young—*Live Fast, Love Hard, Die Young*—and Jordan couldn't make out what he said. Marisol, of course, didn't respond. She kept plucking those empties like weeds from the garden. Hobie said something else, put one hand on her back, the other up her shirt, went in for a kiss. Altus watched it all go down, eyes flooded with booze. He might as well have been watching it happen to strangers on a television screen.

Jordan shoved past him, out of the booth, realized how unsteady she was on her feet. Altus wasn't the only one who'd drank too much.

No matter. Marisol didn't require any help.

She put her hands on either side of Hobie's head, fingers running deep in that oily hair. Marisol let him keep kissing her for a few seconds.

Then she spun his head off like a bottle cap.

Jesus, the blood.

Jordan felt her legs give out, nearly fell but caught herself on the edge of the booth. Hobie's body tumbled off the barstool and onto the floor. Marisol knelt beside him, hands and knees in the blood, slicked her palm with the stuff and put it in her mouth. She looked up at Jordan and her face was nothing but burning white light, a sun in miniature. The other six daughters converged on the body, dug in deep, hand and tooth.

One by one, their faces lit up like stars.

Jordan realized she was walking toward them, lured by the light.

Not for the first time, Jordan considered that living in this place was like being thrown in the deep end of the pool, where her feet couldn't touch.

Hell of a thing though, she was learning to swim.

Mother, mother, mother.

Jordan sat down next to what remained of Hobie, the blood hot on her hands and soaking her clothes. The sisters pressed in around her, invited her into their communion. Bloody grins split their faces ear to ear. Jordan felt like she was on fire, and she wasn't sure if the heat was coming from their burning faces, or from somewhere inside herself. The bar was gone, and night spun around her in a slow, hazy circle. The stars above were alive and pulsing, and the moon was thin, like the blade of a knife. A drone, low and eternal, settled into her bones, into her teeth. She pressed her eyes closed, afraid the light screaming off the seven daughters might blind her. But there was no fear. No uncertainty. They didn't mean Jordan any harm. The daughters lifted her up, twirled her about in the forever dark, leading her along in a dance as old as the universe itself. Jordan laughed, drank deep, tasted copper in her throat. The blood was alive, and the blood was all that mattered. Every shitty choice Jordan had made, every one that had been forced upon her, they'd all been worth it. They'd all brought her to this place, right here, right now. The women were singing, and the song was meant only for her. They hadn't come down from the heavens because Altus called them.

They were here for Jordan.

They were here to answer her prayers.

I didn't find you by accident.

When everything around her eventually stilled, Jordan worked up the nerve to open her eyes. The bar was back, and she was alone. No Altus. No seven daughters. Hobie's remains had gone cold.

How long had she been out?

She stumbled over to the house, found Altus in bed and crawled under the covers beside him, sticky with blood and drunk on impossibilities. Altus kept his distance, tried to pretend he was asleep.

Jordan laughed, closed her eyes.

Dreamed about her daughters.

✳

Jordan slept all through the next day, woke to a dying red sliver of sun sneaking in between the curtain and the windowsill. She got up, showered. Threw her things into her duffle and headed out past the gas pumps to the highway. She stood deep in the darkness with nothing but blue swaths of starlight overhead. The old restlessness had settled back in, but Jordan understood herself better now. Understood a whole lot of things that had puzzled her before. The wind lifted granules of sand, scattered them against the bar's aluminum roof with a clatter. Roughneck Roost heaved and sighed, leaning and broken and giving way to the elements. The yellowed sign was dark, and the bar was padlocked. This blasted spot of earth had been forgotten by every living thing. The seven daughters had gone away sometime in the night. Jordan could feel their absence in the way reality had firmed up around her. There was no mystery left here, just a brittle, dying landscape she couldn't wait to escape. Altus was here somewhere, but Jordan didn't figure she owed him a goodbye, and she was pretty sure he was keeping himself hidden until she left.

Jordan hit the highway, started walking. Five miles to the interstate and then she'd find a way to deal with whatever came at her next.

She always did.

A new constellation burned white in the sky, seven stars—*seven daughters*—sent to guide her way. Jordan knew they wouldn't lead her astray. They might have raided her secrets, but last night they'd left her some of their own. Tattoos chased themselves up and down Jordan's arms, complex patterns that told her everything she needed to know about where she'd been, and where she was going.

This is the beginning of everything.

Something squirmed inside her, kicked.

Mother, mother, mother.

Well, it was definitely the beginning of *something.*

THE GREEN REALM

Part One: What Is

Clayton has nothing left but the tape, so he presses it into the VHS deck, hits play, and loses himself in the forest again. A low-res procession of trees sweeps across the surface of his flatscreen, their leaves crisped brown by the summer heat. Sunlight flares against the lens and the image lights up Clayton's dark apartment. A younger version of himself comes into focus, grins at the camera, chases after the others. Edie's laugh is mired in static, too close to the microphone. It kills Clayton every time he hears it. Edie is the one with the camcorder. A graduation gift from her grandmother. She wanted to be a filmmaker. An actress. She wanted to be anything really, so long as she could be somewhere else.

The image shudders, and Clayton holds his breath. Maybe that ancient tape is finally going to snap. But it keeps going, the forest comes back into view, and Edie is laughing again, yelling for everyone to slow the fuck down so she can catch up. That younger Clayton shifts his blue canvas backpack from one shoulder to the other, looks over the top of his gas station Ray Bans and tells her not to fall too far behind, because Old Sam will eat her up like a slice of pizza, and the younger Clayton's voice is an alien thing to the man in the Houston high-rise, stirring his fourth Bloody Mary of the morning with a wilted celery stalk. It sounds like an echo of who he used to be. Maybe the last time his voice was so confident, so untroubled.

The camera zooms over the younger Clayton's shoulder, finds Scott with his tongue out, throwing up devil horns with both hands. Julie pushes Scott's long black hair back over his shoulder and plants a kiss on his cheek. Edie's voice, still loud in the microphone, tells Clayton that she doesn't have to outrun Old Sam, she just has to outrun his slow ass, and all four teenagers start to laugh.

The camera zooms out. Young Clayton grins. He turns and trots up a weedy slope toward the spot where Julie and Scott are holding hands, swinging their arms like they're still at Marcy Elementary, playing Red Rover at recess. The camera moves to Clayton's back, down to his butt, zooms in fuzzy and close. Edie yells *ooh, la, la* and starts to cackle. The Clayton in the Houston high-rise closes his eyes, thinks about time travel. Tries to wish himself back into his younger form. He ignores the angry sound of Maribeth, slamming drawers and shoving her things into a pair of roller bag suitcases. Clayton has lost everything before, more than once. Clayton is having a hard time feeling anything about the breakup at all. He opens his eyes, won't look away from what's coming next.

The camera lurches as Edie jogs to catch up. Clayton feels the tomato juice and vodka roil in his stomach. The camera lens pitches downward, back up. Teenagers goof around against a backdrop of longleaf pines. Scott chugs water from a Boy Scout canteen. Julie digs in her backpack for the bug spray.

Then a sound freezes the teens in place. Birds flush from the upper tree branches. The sound carries in from the depths of the forest like a foghorn across the water. An animal growl. Low, resonant. Coming from everywhere at once. Terrifying in the moment, and louder than any animal should be. This sound, captured on a VHS tape, still rumbles like the end of the world through Clayton's surround sound.

Maribeth shouts something from the bedroom. Clayton can't hear what she's saying. Doesn't know if it matters at this point.

The growl fades, and the only sound on the tape is the teens' heavy breathing. Scott asks *What the fuck?* and Julie hushes him, puts a hand on his shoulder and peers deeper into the woods.

For real, what was that? Scott's voice sounds like it's coming from underwater. Clayton has watched this tape so many times it's becoming threadbare, the quality diminished.

Maribeth yells something else on her way out the door.

Clayton turns up the sound, thinks about rewinding to hear that guttural growl again. He hates the quiet part.

Ten seconds of silence, then Julie whispers, her voice far too serious. *Y'all. I think that was Old Sam.*

And the way she says it, that's enough to break the tension. The teens double over with laughter. The camera spins around as Edie moves to turn it off. Like always, Clayton wishes she'd caught at least a glimpse of herself as she did this, but the lens never found her. He remembers everything about that day, but the older he gets, the more elusive Edie becomes. With the tape, he can always reset Julie and Scott in his memory, but Edie is nothing but black and white yearbook photographs anymore.

The tape ends. The screen goes blue.

Those kids are close to Campsite 11. Just a half mile or so, and they'll pitch camp.

But the version of Clayton with too many miles on him sees something they never noticed. That last shot, right as Julie starts to speak? There's something in the trees. A good twenty yards away, but no farther. A shape like a man, but tall. Maybe dark and furred with arms all the way to the ground, or just a blurry play of shadows and underbrush on a really old fucking video tape. Maybe it's a deer or a bear, or maybe it's something else.

Clayton has studied it a thousand times, and still can't say for sure.

✳

Clayton leaves Houston on I-45.

He brought the vodka with him, left the mixer behind. Heat pulses off the concrete and the daylight is blinding.

The backseat of his white Tesla is crowded with all the camping gear he could salvage. It belongs to Maribeth, stuff she hasn't carried off yet. Maribeth loves the outdoors. Likes to backpack on vacation, likes to go horseback riding and deep-sea fishing. Clayton is decidedly an indoors type. Prefers his nature confined to documentaries. This incompatibility isn't the only reason Maribeth is moving in with some guy from her office, but it certainly hasn't drawn them any closer.

Beyond the metro, the pine trees overtake the world.

Clayton sweats through his shirt. Cranks up the AC.

If he had his way, the cities would swallow up every tree in Texas.

Clayton tells himself he isn't fleeing the latest implosion in his life. And he's absolutely *not* hunting for Old Sam. Rather, he is finally resigned to finding some answers. Every time he drives up to Dallas for a deposition or a client consult, he passes that exit south of Huntsville that leads to the dark sprawl of the Sam Houston National Forest, and Campsite 11. Clayton isn't sure how to restart his life yet again, and simply watching the VHS tape alone in the dark over and over has become untenable. Still, going back to Campsite 11 feels foolish and dangerous.

But there's so much he needs to know.

And if he doesn't show up at the firm on Monday? Will anyone really care?

Unlikely.

Clayton has a teenaged daughter named Lexi, who might miss him, though he only sees her a couple times a year. She lives in Florida with Clayton's first ex-wife, Hannah Dawn, who lives with a man named Clutch. Clutch is fond of sleeveless tees and rebel flag tattoos, and he owns half the car lots in Gainesville. Clutch wears a thirty-eight in a holster, and claims to have enemies. Clutch always rides along with Hannah Dawn when she meets Clayton in Mobile to hand off Lexi and her suitcase for one of her visits. This halfway point swap makes Clayton feel kind of seedy, like he's conducting some sort of illicit business. Clutch always gives Lexi a bear hug before she goes, like he wants to show Clayton who her *real* Daddy is. If Clayton was worth a shit, he'd figure a way to get custody of Lexi. But he's not sure he'd be a better father than the sorta one she has in Gainesville.

Clayton takes the correct exit without thinking, the way to the campground still strong in his memory.

He drives for a bit, passes a falling down wooden church nearly swallowed up by the brush. A few more turns, another few minutes, and the Tesla pulls into a gravel parking lot that's cracked and mostly overrun with weeds and debris. Flattened beer cans, plastic bags latched onto tree limbs. A Styrofoam cooler, snapped in half and filled with spider webs. There used to be a sign pointing out the path to the campsites, but now there's only a splintered wooden post with brown paint peeling away.

This was the place, though. No doubt about it.

Julie had found this site, of course. Deep in the woods. Clayton is certain he's alone. He unloads the gear, hating the humidity. He wears cargo pants, a V-neck tee, tennis shoes. Clayton is not overly prepared. But he manages the heavy backpack, and the tent is bound in a drawstring bag that's easy to carry. No delaying. Clayton leaves the parking lot and follows the overgrown path into the woods.

✳

Clayton learns there is no such thing as time travel.

His younger self followed this path through the forest with youthful strides, leaping about, walking backwards, mugging for the camera. For the Clayton of today, it's a sweaty, heart-testing slog. His gray hair clings to his forehead, and gnats buzz around his ears. Clayton wishes he'd worn a cap. Clayton wishes he'd spent more time on the elliptical. Sharp bladed palmettos have invaded the path, and they catch against his every step.

He doesn't remember Campsite 11 being so far from the parking lot, but as he trudges along, he does remember the curious fact that there were no other campsites along the way. No Campsite one through ten. No campsites twelve and up. Just a casual walk through the forest, punctuated by the bloodcurdling sound of *whatever* they'd heard, and then a brown sign on a post with a gold painted number eleven.

Clayton is so tired of mysteries.

He's carried the weight of not knowing things for too fucking long, and he's losing strength.

The pines grow so tight against the path, Clayton feels like he's being squeezed to death. Tree frogs bark and insects sing. No wind cuts this deep through the forest, and everything is still. It feels like time is winding down and the world is slowing. The air is wet and suffocating. Clayton's feet ache and his left knee begins to complain with the usual stabbing pain. Clayton huffs and puffs along, certain he'll recognize the spot where they heard that animal growl, but everything has changed. If someone kept the path cleared back in the day, that someone has retired. Clayton is surprised to see the sign for Campsite 11 appear as if by magic, not ten feet ahead of him, the golden eleven freshly painted, the post sticking up from knee high grass. He drops everything he's carrying and sits long enough to catch his breath.

Clayton doesn't dwell on his memories of Campsite 11.

Not yet.

Instead, he fumbles the tent together, all the while wishing Maribeth was there to help. Clayton envisions a scenario wherein he informs her he's willing to try harder, to put away all his *could have beens* and focus on *could bes*, but he knows himself better than that. He's never lived in the present. Not for very long, anyway. He didn't bring a hammer, so he stomps the stakes into the soft ground with his shoe and hopes they'll hold if the wind picks up. The stillness is so heavy, it's hard to breathe. He thinks it would be about right for him to die out here of a heart attack. Part of him belongs here. He doesn't know why he was allowed to leave in the first place.

The forest is lifeless and still, but Clayton knows how quickly it can come alive. The tent constructed, he sits down in the dirt, huffing and puffing, unconcerned with fire ants or copperheads. What does it matter? He's pretty sure there used to be benches here, but they're long gone. Night races in, and Clayton waits for something to happen. He waits for his friends to call out from the darkness, to come pitch a tent beside his. He waits for a low rumbling call from the heart of the forest to announce the arrival of the answers he's been seeking.

Clayton waits.

Part 2: What Was

The Caprice Classic belonged to Julie's Mom, and they borrowed it for the road trip because the AC blew cold, and they all drove junkers that would have left them stranded along the highway before they reached the next county. Julie wouldn't let anyone else drive, and she kept the needle right at fifty-five the whole way. Scott rode shotgun, and commanded the tape deck, which meant nothing but glam metal and seventies stoner rock for four hundred miles. That was fine with Clayton. He spread out in the back seat and kept a low buzz going most of the way. Edie reached into the cooler full of half-melted ice that sat between them on the bench seat, pulled out cans of Keystone Light to pass around. Everyone drank but Julie. She was straight edge and on a mission. Edie cracked the window so she could let out her cigarette smoke. Her dark hair was cut short and choppy, and her aviator shades caught the mottled reflection of the endless pines along the highway.

The four of them grew up in a small West Texas town, and they'd never seen so many trees. The pines made Clayton nervous. Back home, the horizons hid nothing, and he couldn't help but wonder what lived in the depths of all that green. He took another drink, grimaced at how crazy he felt. Either he was more buzzed than he thought, or Julie was starting to get to him. She always carried around paperback books with titles like *Strange but True Ghostly Encounters* and *World's Most Terrifying Phenomenon: Uncovered!* She'd brought along a stack of them, and Edie dug one up from the floorboard, started flipping through pages. This one was called *Lone Star Terrors: True Tales of Texas Monsters.* And Julie being Julie, she'd bookmarked certain pages, highlighted key passages in yellow, so Edie turned right to the good parts.

She tossed her cigarette butt out the window and kicked the back of Julie's seat. "Hey, Jules. This says Old Sam is like eight feet tall with arms that touch his toes. And everyone who's seen him says he smells like a sewer. Why is it again you want to go looking for this thing?"

Julie kept both hands on the wheel. "Because I want to know if he's real."

"I really hope he's not," said Clayton.

"But what if we were the ones to discover him?" asked Julie. "You don't think that would be cool?"

"If he looks anything like the drawing in this book," said Edie, "I don't want to be anywhere near him."

"Y'all are just chickenshit." Scott sat in the passenger seat with his Reeboks on the dash and the sleeves cut off his Dokken tee shirt. His jeans were shredded so bad, more skin was visible than denim.

"Like you wouldn't shit your pants if he came shaking your tent," said Clayton.

"Oh, yeah," said Scott. "Probably would. But that don't mean I couldn't take him if he squared up."

"Didn't Julie kick your ass in middle school?"

"True story," said Julie. "He spilled a full Dr. Pepper on my math homework."

"I've grown some since then," said Scott.

Laughter infected the car, momentarily chased away the bleak certainty growing inside Clayton that this would be the last time they were ever this close again. They were six weeks out of high school, neck deep in the last real summer of their lives. The last one that *felt* like summer, anyway. They were headed in different directions. Edie to Los Angeles. Scott up to Lubbock, for a job with his uncle's auto body shop. Julie off to some east coast school where she'd probably wind up with a few advanced degrees and a six-figure job. And Clayton's parents had long ago determined he'd become a lawyer, so his bags were already packed for The University of Houston, whether he wanted to leave or not.

Clayton never considered his hometown a place anyone stayed. More like a place you fled.

Still, the feeling they were all fleeing in different directions was too much for him to take.

So, Clayton squirmed in the backseat, clung to the road trip like a life raft. He didn't give a fuck about hunting forest monsters. He just wanted to savor these last days together. Spend some time exploring Houston and maybe checking out one of those giant fucking malls. But Julie was insistent. If they were coming all this way, they were damn sure going to explore these woods. Everyone seemed excited, even Edie, so Clayton went with the flow. Small price to pay for a week of them all together.

"Right turn, Clyde," said Scott.

"Huh?" said Julie.

"Here, exit right here."

Scott had a roadmap spread out over half the dashboard, and beer sloshed over the rumpled face of it as he motioned with his can, toward the exit.

"Oh shit," said Julie. "Don't spill it on the seats."

Julie made the exit, and a few minutes later, she steered them onto a park road that stabbed into the heart of the forest. She referred to a sun-faded pamphlet they'd picked up from a gas station spinner rack in Huntsville, and after a seemingly endless drive through the woods, she pulled into a gravel parking lot bound by repurposed wooden railroad ties.

"Everybody grab your stuff." When Julie turned off the ignition, the Caprice ticked and moaned in the heat.

"This is the campsite?" Clayton asked.

"About a mile that way." Julie pointed toward a well-trod path that disappeared into the trees. A sign stood at the trailhead, displaying a faded park map behind a sheet of scratched and weathered Plexiglass.

"Wait, we have to hike?"

"The campsite is in the woods. This is as close as the road goes. Don't be a wuss, it's not far."

"They got wolves and shit out here?" asked Scott.

"I don't think so," said Julie.

"What about bears?"

"No bears," said Edie. "Old Sam already ate those motherfuckers for breakfast."

Eager to proceed, Julie led them onto the trail.

Shadows collapsed on top of them. The sun was still up there, somewhere, sneaking looks through the canopy, but the arboreal embrace unsettled Clayton, left him peering up in search of a vanished sky. Pine needles crunched beneath his tennis shoes, and quiet birdsong drifted down from the treetops. Heat hugged the ground. Somewhere beyond the shimmery surface of the path, tree limbs bent and snapped with the movement of unseen life. Insects chittered from the undergrowth. The forest seemed to Clayton like it was engaged in a conversation of its own, far beyond the understanding of four teenagers teetering on the edge of a new, terrifying existence.

Scott wore a Walkman on his belt, with the headphones hung around his neck. Volume cranked so loud, the tinny sound of George Lynch unleashing a hellacious guitar solo became part of the forest song.

"So how do you hunt for a bigfoot?" he asked.

Julie had twice as much shit in her backpack as everyone else, no doubt prepared for every eventuality. She shifted the weight on her shoulders, marching stridently along the path. Powered by the same unfailing drive that ensured straight As and bright futures. "You just walk around and look, I guess."

"Wait, you don't have a ten-step plan?" said Scott. "No spiral bound notebook precisely filled with color coded ink?"

"What do you want? All my highlighters ran dry."

"None of your monster books say anything about it?"

"There's no manual for bigfoot hunting, dude."

"If there was, you'd definitely own a copy."

"Please feel free to fuck off, Scott."

Theirs was a playful argument. They were all smiles. Enlivened by their love.

Clayton felt a surge of jealousy. Scott and Julie were closer to one another than he'd ever been to anyone.

Edie threw an arm around Clayton's shoulder, pulled him into a conspiratorial hug. She smelled like coconut shampoo and spilled beer.

Clayton shivered. Felt the sweaty warmth of her arm against the back of his neck. Edie had the camera in her other hand, keeping it level on Scott and Julie as they trudged along. Edie spoke to whatever audience might one day watch her video. Voice mock serious, like she was narrating a nature program.

"Two young assholes, captured on tape in their not exactly natural habitat."

"I'm only kind of an asshole," said Julie.

"What about you, Scott?" Edie adjusted the camera, started to pull away. Clayton let his arm circle her back, breathless at his own bravery.

"One hundred percent pure," said Scott.

"See how they caper and strut," said Edie. "Engaged in the ancient mating ritual of their kind. Shit talking."

"Not shit talking." Scott called back over his shoulder, hurrying to keep pace with Julie. "More like foreplay."

"Keep wishing," said Julie.

Edie laughed, and Clayton became caught up in her joy.

Even when she pulled away and turned the camera toward his face, his smile stayed true. Already he missed the weight of her against him, but seeing himself reflected in her lens made him feel just as close to her.

"It's time for your closeup." Edie zoomed in on Clayton's face, and he mugged for the camera. Making monkey faces. Peeking over the top of his shades like Tom Cruise on the Risky Business poster. Wondering if Edie thought he was remotely cool. Then a stench blossomed in the heat, like sewage and spoiled meat. Like milk that's gone solid in the carton. Edie recoiled. Let the camera lens ease down toward the ground. Clayton pulled his tee shirt collar up over his nose, wondered for a second if he might throw up, right there in front of his friends. Edie watched him, face knotted in disgust. Like she thought maybe Clayton was the source of the horrible smell.

"What in the fuck?" said Scott. "Do y'all smell that?"

"Obviously," said Edie. "Julie, is this campsite of yours near a junkyard or something."

"Wait, your books said the monster stinks, yeah?" Scott was grinning ear to ear, despite the knee-buckling stench. "Oh shit, he's coming for us."

"Yeah, that's probably it," said Clayton.

Edie was still looking at him, but he'd never been good at guessing her thoughts.

"Let's find him first." Clayton jogged toward Scott and Julie, waving for Edie to follow. Desperate to reclaim the moment of closeness between them that had passed. Terrified to stand still too long beneath the questing weight of her regard. He understood with great clarity there was no path to Edie's affection that didn't require him to *talk to her about it.* To just ask how she felt, and lay his heart wide open in the process. It was the way of things. But he waited for a revelation that never came. Hoping, perhaps, she'd offer some overwhelming signal to proceed with his desires.

Clayton jogged backward, waving, and grinning at Edie, putting on a show for the camera.

Well aware what a coward he was.

"Slow the fuck down," said Edie. "Let me catch up."

"Don't fall behind," said Clayton. "Old Sam will eat you up like a slice of pizza."

"I don't have to outrun Old Sam," she said, "just your slow ass."

Everyone laughed. Clayton caught up with Scott and Julie, heard Edie calling from behind. *Ooh, la, la.* Looked back and saw she had the camera on him again. He wished for time travel. Just to fast forward to a place where they were living somewhere together in California, no questions left between them. Maybe Edie was a movie star. Maybe Clayton was anything other than a lawyer. They'd have a little girl named Lexi because Edie had a baby doll with that name when she was a kid, and always talked about how that's what she'd call her daughter, when she had one. Their lives would be nothing but palm trees and sunshine and endless summers together.

They pulled up to wait for Edie. Scott chugged lukewarm water from the canteen he took to scout camp when he and Clayton joined up back in middle school. Scott made it to First Class. Clayton never got past Tenderfoot. But they were both in it long enough to figure maybe they weren't cut out for wilderness activities. As if to drive home the point, mosquitoes appeared in a sudden swarm, causing Julie to produce a can of bug spray from her pack and cover every inch of them in the sticky, smelly stuff. Clayton's feet hurt—tennis shoes probably weren't the best choice for this sort of hike—and his clothes clung tight with sweat. He longed for the air conditioning back in the Caprice, wondered, as he had at scout camp, why in the world anyone would subject themselves to the great outdoors.

Edie caught up. Got a bug repellant bath.

And then a howl stopped them all cold.

It was guttural. Deep and rumbling, like something heavy was moving through the forest. So loud, it was easy to imagine the displacement of air, pushing through the trees and slamming into your chest. And there was an underlying wetness to the sound. Throaty and vile. Clayton had never experienced wild animals, outside *Mutual of Omaha's Wild Kingdom* on Saturday afternoons, but he felt certain that whatever called to them was outside the range of normal human experience. An animal couldn't sound like that. Couldn't be so loud. And worst of all, there was a high keening sound that accompanied the howl, an underlying shriek that was almost beyond the human frequency. It put Clayton in mind of the banshee, a creature he'd read about in one of Julie's books that heralded death with just that sort of unsettling scream.

Tears flooded Clayton's eyes. He hurried to wipe them away with his forearm.

The howl lingered for another few seconds, then faded.

All the forest noises had fled. The world became so quiet that Clayton imagined he could hear his friends' terrified heartbeats. In that moment, the silence was almost worse than the howling.

Disembodied and hollow. Ready to fracture into chaos.

"What the fuck?" said Scott.

"Hush," said Julie. "Listen."

Edie scanned the woods with her camera. Clayton began wondering just how much truth might be contained in Julie's stupid books.

"For real," said Scott. "What was that?"

Julie held the can of bug spray out in front of her, as if it might defend them from whatever stalked the woods. The foul stench that preceded the howling began to recede, but the presence of something heavy and menacing remained. They stood knotted together, afraid to move, expecting something terrible, but unsure what form it would take. Clayton could hear the tape moving in Edie's camcorder. Could hear the gurgling sound of his stomach, rebelling against all the beer he'd drunk.

"Y'all. I think that was Old Sam." Julie's voice was hushed. Earnest. Scott barked a laugh. Tried and failed to hold back another. Edie caught it too, began pealing with laughter. They all joined in, even Julie. Doubled over at the pure absurdity of the moment. As if summoned by their joy, the birds returned to the trees and frogs began chirping from the brush. Edie turned off the camera, packed it away. Convinced it was a pain in the ass to film every step of their adventure. Scott passed around his canteen, and they argued over whether the howl came from a bear, a wolf, or something supernatural. Nobody could say for sure. But in the end, there was nothing to do but proceed to Campsite 11, and wait for night to descend. According to Julie's book, Old Sam was more active at night. Emboldened by what she considered a close encounter with the beast, Julie set a vigorous pace through the woods. The rest of them did their best to keep up, laughing and joking and complaining about the heat, as the shadows deepened, and the trees closed in.

*

One of the only things Clayton recalled fondly from his time in the Boy Scouts was the campfire. In particular, the lazy heat that never seemed to offend, even on the hottest night, and the comfortable smell of wood-smoke. Where he grew up, they seemed always to burn mesquite, but Campsite 11 had been stocked with pine, and it produced an exotic scent that caused Clayton to feel far removed from his youth. This was the smell of *someplace else*. The burning heart of the beckoning world. His eyes watered and his face was hot. The few beers they'd stashed in their packs were too warm to enjoy much. But Scott fashioned a bong from a Dr. Pepper can, and after the can had circumnavigated the fire a few times, everyone but Julie was feeling the effects.

They took a stab at cooking bacon in an aluminum pan, and finally settled for the cheese slices and bread they'd brought for the walk back the next day. Campsite 11 was nothing more than a clearing in the woods. A pair of wooden benches on opposite sides of a grated firepit. A perimeter large enough to contain their three tents, but otherwise at the mercy of the wilderness. Yet together, seated around the fire, they formed an impenetrable unit, untroubled by anything living in the deep blackness of the forest.

"Really love being the only one not stoned." Julie held a piece of bread close to the flames, like toasting it might spice up the otherwise dull meal.

"Yeah, sucks for you." Scott kissed her on the cheek. Tossed the corpse of the Dr. Pepper can onto the grate and watched it blacken.

"So how long before Old Sam shows up?" said Edie.

"Funny," said Julie. "Let me know if you can explain away that howl."

"I'm with Jules," said Clayton. "That wasn't a normal animal. Sounded like a fucking monster to me."

"You were always my favorite, Clayton." Julie grinned, tore her piece of toast in half and gave part to him.

"I'm everyone's favorite," he said, mouth full of dry bread. "It's because I'm so lovable. And good looking."

Scott side armed a stale slice of cheese in Clayton's direction. "You do all you can with such limited resources. I'll give you that."

"Dude, quit throwing shit," he said.

"Listen," said Edie. "Jules is obviously everyone's favorite. There's no contest. Brave as fuck monster hunter. Celebrated campfire chef. And the only one smart enough not to get stoned in the woods with a bunch of idiots."

"Hard to argue," said Scott.

Julie grinned. "Okay, Edie. Maybe *you're* my favorite."

It was the same sort of playful ribbing they'd shared since elementary school. Youthful and eternal. They formed a core at the back of Mrs. Richardson's second grade class, and it held together through the years, unbroken by any challengers. On occasion, someone else would try to infiltrate. A supplemental friend, like the summer Leticia Redding started hanging around, hoping to get a date with Scott. Or the Bronson brothers who worked at the movie theater with Edie, always showing up with six packs and tabs of acid. But no one hung around for long. Girlfriends, boyfriends. Those relationships were all short-lived. No outside force could threaten the harmony of their cabal.

For years, Clayton blamed this communal closeness for the way he hated every guy Edie dated.

Eventually, he figured out he was in love with her.

Clayton settled into a comfortable buzz, floated away on their laughter as it travelled around the campfire. He imagined a feral existence where none of them ever left; instead, they lived free forever in the midnight woods, foraging for mushrooms and stalking wild game. Eyes alive with reflected firelight. An existence where Campsite 11 became their whole world, and never mind the rest of it. If they stayed, truly nothing could pull them apart. No parents or life demands. No uncertain futures. Someone would come looking for them eventually, but they'd never be found. Just the haunting memory of four best friends, torn loose from the real world, but still wild and alive in a primeval forest. A beautiful green realm, protected by Old Sam and his mysteries. Clayton and his friends had been allowed entrance into the monster's kingdom. Now Old Sam and his ilk would protect them. Frighten the world away. As much as Clayton knew it was impossible, as much as he *hated* the woods, his thoughts ran desperate, and he wished for an eternity in that moment.

Beyond the camp perimeter sparked tiny lights.

Fireflies. Will-o-the wisp. Blinking animal eyes, searing white. Watching from the trees.

And howls. Not so close. Not so unplaceable. But howls, nonetheless, moving like fog across the landscape.

"I'm going to sleep," said Julie. "Maybe get up early and see if Old Sam likes the mornings better."

She stood, held her hand out to Scott. He took it, rose, and stretched with a theatrical yawn.

"Guess that's me too," he said. "Sleep tight."

They retired to their tent, laughing and enamored. So sure of one another. Perfectly certain their love would survive the ravages of geography. Clayton feared for them. Clayton lived in the real world, no matter how hard he tried to escape it. High school kids who move across the country from one another rarely make relationships stick, no matter how tight they were. And if Julie and Scott crumbled, there was no hope for any of them. The melancholy that had chased Clayton the whole trip found him again, settled in his chest like a cancer. Almost imperceptibly, he leaned toward Edie, so close together their shoulders touched, and he could feel her hair tickling his cheek.

Edie put a hand on top of his, and the rickety bench shifted beneath them. They drifted in the silence together, probing the yawning divide between friendship and something else.

"So, Old Sam," said Edie. "You believe that shit?"

Clayton shook his head. Old Sam was suddenly the last thing on his mind. "Not really. But it's fun to pretend, I guess?"

"For Julie's sake?" said Edie.

"For all out sakes, I think."

"What do you mean?"

"Enjoy the adventure, I guess? We're all having fun with the idea of Old Sam. Doesn't matter if he's real. This might be the last time we can all goof around together."

"You think that?"

"Don't you?"

"I mean, it doesn't *have* to be."

And Clayton knew she was right. Nothing had to be.

Every possibility existed in that moment.

Edie turned toward him, still holding his hand, her eyes as unreadable as ever. The forest sang. Mysteries moved through the shadows. A line of sweat streaked down Edie's temple. She was so close to Clayton now, the world circled around them, but they remained still in the center of it all, trapped in the eye of the moment. Clayton focused on the slight curl of Edie's smile, and anticipated what it might mean. The trees grew soft around them. Streaky at the edges. The orange campfire bled away into the sky. And Clayton could hear huge, lumbering things in the woods. Impossible things that could not sway them from their sudden act of discovery. Edie's smile broadened. Clayton's heart hammered so hard, he felt he might lose his breath. White flashes appeared, like a sea of twinkling stars through the trees. Billowing blue smoke, stirred in the air. But Clayton paid his surroundings no mind. None of it was real.

Only Edie and her smile.

Only his dreams taking tangible form.

"Is there something here?" she asked.

Edie might have meant *something lurking in the forest,* or she might have meant a *long-hidden affection revealing itself.*

Clayton couldn't say for sure, so he answered, "I hope so," which addressed either question.

Clayton drew closer to her. So close he could feel the bug spray on her legs sticking to his. So close he could smell the green, woody scent of the forest on her clothes.

"What are you doing, huh?" she said.

"I'm sorry. I'm really not sure."

Edie put a hand on the back of his neck, pulled him close until their foreheads touched. "A couple of years ago, this would have been a better idea."

"It's still a pretty good one, I think."

"You know I'm still going to California?"

"Yeah."

"All right then."

Edie kissed him. They were both sweaty and reeling from the smoke. Stoned and lonely in the shimmering forest. And the kiss lasted long enough for Clayton to redirect the course of his life.

There would be no Houston. No law school.

There would only be California bliss with Edie.

This kiss was the line of demarcation between the boy he'd been and the person he would become. Edie and Clayton would be an unbreakable duo. Not like his parents, who barely spoke except to scold one another. Not like Edie's parents, whose violent divorce torched any hope she had for a safe and comfortable childhood. Edie and Clayton would twine together like wisps of woodsmoke. One person. Alive and running. Battling the world together, forever young. Everything Clayton ever dreamed of came alive in that instant, and he drew Edie in tight, afraid she'd pull away. Afraid the whole thing really was a dream.

When Edie did pull away, she was still smiling. Her eyes were as unreadable as always, but Clayton believed he saw a lifeline in her expression.

"I'm high as fuck, Clayton. I gotta go to sleep."

"Can I come?" he asked.

"I like you, dude. But I'm not about to fuck you out here in the forest."

That got them both laughing. Edie kissed him again, this time fleeting and soft. Then she stood, still holding on to one hand, studied him like she was trying to read his mind. Her brow furrowed, and Clayton wondered if she found him inscrutable in the same way he found her. Maybe they were both more confident in their loneliness than in their ability to connect.

Firelight backlit Edie's beauty. Long howls penetrated the night. Those flickering lights moved from white to green to gold. They haunted the periphery of Clayton's vision, like coaxing invitations to some other world. But Edie commanded his attention. He watched her move away from him, abandoning the moment in favor of sleep. Clayton was desperate to know what she was thinking, what she was *feeling*. He watched her regress into the darkness, toward her haphazardly assembled tent.

The night crowded it. Nearly swallowed her whole.

"Edie?"

She waved goodnight as she crawled into her tent, but she didn't look back. "We have time to figure stuff out, Clayton. Not tonight, though. Tired. Sleep. Now."

And of course, she was right.

Not every mystery had to be solved tonight.

So, Clayton sat by the fire. Until the lights faded, and the forest grew still. Until the logs burned to ash. And when he finally crawled into his tent, he lay on top of his sleeping bag, imagining every possible future, and fretting over none of them.

Edie was his best friend. Maybe the love of his life.

Together, they were unstoppable.

And they had the rest of their lives to figure things out.

Part 3: What Will Be

Mysteries will abide.

A Tesla will be discovered, parked near the trailhead. Registered to some high-priced Houston lawyer. Empty bottle of vodka overturned in the passenger seat. Deeper in the woods, a ruined tent, caught up in the brush, anchored to the earth by a lone stake. A clearing that used to be a campground, overgrown and long since abandoned. People will remark on the peculiar silence of the place. Of the deep and harrowing sense of loneliness that pervades. Those of a certain mindset will recognize a liminal resonance, a thin seam in reality through which they might venture, were they brave enough. None of them will be. None of them will remain there long. They will feel as if they're being watched. Being *sought out*, in a way. The former campsite will be abandoned to the mercies of the forest. Shunned by even the woodland animals.

Only the silence will remain, unbroken by howl or shriek or youthful laughter.

No reason will remain to visit that place.

Possibilities used to exist there.

But any *hope* that dwelled in that darkness will have long since departed.

TILL THE GREENTEETH DRAW US DOWN

After the greenteeth took our parents, me and Squirrel moved in with Lady Lucy, who owned a bookstore before the water came and turned most of her inventory to muck. Lady Lucy had moved as many books as she could to her upstairs apartment, left her most prized volumes to dry out on the windowsill in the sunshine before shelving them in the various nooks and crannies she'd previously used to store alarm clocks and oven mitts and other things she no longer had use for. Squirrel called her Lady Lucifer behind her back, because our benefactor grew cold and cruel every time she drank blackberry wine. She'd indulge in bitter tirades about how lucky we were to be children because we hadn't enough hard life experience to draw the greenteeth to us. But I knew that was bullshit. I was living proof that despair didn't wait for old age.

Black clouds squatted low against the city on the day Squirrel went missing. Cold rain splattered the windows, and we lounged around Lady Lucy's cave of moldy books, imagining summer days when we might swim through the saltwater streets and dive from the third-story windows of beach hotels. Lady Lucy searched an hour for her copy of *Dandelion Wine* before remembering she'd loaned it out in exchange for a dry pack of Marlboro Reds and a book of matches. It's how Lady Lucy supported herself, and us. A one-week loan of a mostly intact copy of *Beowulf* could be had for a few unexpired cans of cream corn. Or maybe you wanted to borrow her copy of *Lonesome Dove*. That would cost you a six-pack of bottled Dasani water for the pleasure. Ever since the hurricane cut through Galveston and the waters refused to withdraw, entertainment was at a premium. So, Lady Lucy had quite a racket going, and we all benefitted.

Me and Squirrel had the run of her shelves, and she constantly shoved books in our hands, telling us we *simply must* read this or that.

"You've read *Cat's Cradle*, haven't you, Rowdy?" she'd ask. I'd say no, and she'd climb up on a tottering stool and pull down a copy. One day she gave me a soggy science book, convinced I needed to learn all about how climate change melted the glaciers and raised the sea levels and caused storms—like the one that came through Galveston—to become exponentially more violent. She had a notion that one day I might grow up and figure out a way to reverse all this, but math and science were never my thing, and the book caused my eyes to glaze over.

"Are you hungry, little darlings?" she asked. "Perhaps a tin of Spam?" She always called us *little darlings*, like we were storybook urchins who washed up at her door, which, I suppose, is exactly what we were.

"Yes, please," I answered.

Squirrel ignored the question. She'd spent most of that afternoon with her palms on the window glass, peering into the gloom. The apartment above the drowned bookstore was hardly large enough for one person, let alone three, and the open spaces always called to her. Lady Lucy's rowboat was lashed to the railing of the second-story balcony, bobbing in the swells. Lady's black cat, Bathory, lazed on the windowsill in front of Squirrel. When he heard the lid peel away from the tin of canned meat, Bathory came to life, bolted to the kitchen, and was rewarded with a salty bite from the end of a fork. Lady Lucy portioned out the rest for our meal, looking half a witch with her tangled gray hair, green hooded cloak, and the amiable black cat navigating the space around her ankles. It was an impression she cultivated. And on the day Squirrel and I had arrived at her window, orphaned and alone, she'd joked that it was lucky for us she no longer had a functioning oven, else fairy tale law would demand she cook and eat us.

Lady Lucy was not entirely sane, but I was almost certain she would never eat us.

When we finished our food, she uncorked a bottle of blackberry wine and, as she often did, told stories about Miracle, the woman she'd loved more than anything in the world. Miracle had shared the apartment with Lady Lucy before the storm. They read books to one another by candlelight, stories about lost kingdoms and talking animals and ancient forests full of black-hearted wolves. Lady Lucy often conflated these fictions with their actual time together, though both had lived their whole lives on the island, and there were vanishing few talking animals native to the Texas coast. I was glad she had her fantasies; even imaginary pleasure was better than none. By the Lady's account, Miracle was storybook-beautiful, with the soul of a saint. There was no way to know for sure if Miracle even existed, or if that had really been her name, but it hardly mattered. The storm changed us all. Lady Lucy had been Lucy Brown before. Squirrel was Tina. My parents named me Adam, but now I was Rowdy. Because, why not? If the city could become something new, so could we, and it was easier to forget who we'd all been before than to sit around lamenting what we'd lost.

Lady Lucy finished her story the same as always. "Miracle stood unafraid on that very balcony, night black as a barrel of pitch. She let her hair down long, like a princess imprisoned in a tower. Let the strands rest on the current as she sang sad songs. I watched her without interfering, certain she was going to leave me, and too in love with her to stand in the way. Eventually they came, the greenteeth. They felt her despair and they drew her down to her death. And she was never heard from again."

And she was never heard from again.

The way Lady Lucy spoke the words, it sounded like Miracle was a character in one of her true crime books.

She became quiet after that, just sipped at her wine with heavy eyelids. I read a chapter or two of *American Gods* before growing tired. Bathory lounged in my lap, and we listened to the ocean as it moved through the bones of the city. The sound of the undertow eventually put me to sleep. I woke to black night. Cold air chased in through the open window. I expected to see Squirrel's slim, anxious form still fogging the glass, but she was nowhere in the room, and there was no conclusion to draw other than she'd gone out through the window, into the darkness.

And she was never heard from again.

I roused Lady Lucy from her recliner. She'd fallen asleep too, the empty wine bottle gripped in her hands.

"What has your darling sister done?" Lady Lucy slurred her words, and there was a knife edge to her voice that indicated the wine had taxed her patience.

"She left, I think." I ran over to the window, poked my head out into the drizzle. "The boat's gone. She sailed off somewhere."

"She took my boat?"

"She must have," I said.

"You are certain the greenteeth didn't take her?"

I was certain of nothing, but it made sense that if the greenteeth had drawn her down, she'd have no need for a boat.

I grabbed my jean jacket off the hook, then climbed out the window and onto the balcony. Lady Lucy followed, her billowing hood up against the drizzle. Ocean water lapped at the underside of the balcony. Standing beside the black sea caused my heart to skip. We never went out on the water at night. The despair was too close. The afterlife was too real. The greenteeth were harder to resist. I grabbed the railing to steady myself, leaned out and looked. And there she was. Squirrel with her skinny arms and black tangled curls, chopping into the water with an oar, making steady progress toward the open ocean in Lady Lucy's tiny rowboat.

Lady Lucy grimaced. "Had I a spell for making difficult children vanish, I'd cast it in an instant."

"What?"

"Ignore me," she said. "I'm bitter. We must follow your sister and bring her home."

"How?"

"I'm afraid we'll have to enlist the aid of my would-be suitor."

She meant Mr. Cortez, who lived in the building across the street. His balcony was opposite ours, but crowded with flowerboxes, where he grew yellow squash and green jalapeños that he'd shared with us in the fall. A warped piece of plywood covered his window, and he moved it aside whenever he needed to exit or let the sunlight in. The glass panes had been broken a few months back by a band of teenagers who fancied themselves pirates. They terrorized the neighborhood for months, boating from window to window, smashing glass with baseball bats. Ravaging living rooms for Michelob Light and Slim Jims. Dealing out bruises and broken bones. The rascals tried such an assault on Mr. Cortez, and he met them halfway through the window with his pistol. Put a bullet between one pair of beady pirate eyes. That was enough to send the others paddling away with their lives and nothing more. Lady Lucy jokingly called him Cortez the Killer. She got the name from some old song. That was the last we heard of pirates. They might have continued their crimes, but if so, they'd sailed to another neighborhood.

Lady Lucy called. "Mr. Cortez. Are you awake? We require your assistance."

The plywood board covering his window slid aside, and he peered out. "What's the matter?"

He wore a smashed cowboy hat and a blue pearl-snap shirt. His chin and cheeks were furred with gray, and his skin bore the deep cuts of time. Wrinkles and spots and old-man bruises. But his eyes were friendly, and they shone bright as a lighthouse in a storm every time he saw Lady Lucy.

"One of my little darlings has sailed away, and we need to retrieve her before . . ."

Lady Lucy didn't need to continue. We all understood what came after before. I motioned up the street, and Mr. Cortez saw Squirrel paddling madly, growing smaller every second.

Cortez the Killer did not hesitate.

"We'll take my boat."

He nearly tipped the rowboat over scrambling into it. His long gabardine slacks were tucked into his cowboy boots, like he'd been out walking through the scrub brush.

Old habits, I guess.

Mr. Cortez rowed across to our balcony, helped us into the boat. He smelled of clove cigarettes and sandalwood cologne. He wore his pistol in a leather holster. When we were situated, he shoved off from the balcony with his oar, and Bathory leapt from the railing and positioned himself at the bow. Moonlight painted the water and caught fire in the cat's eyes.

"A cat on a boat brings good luck," said Lady Lucy.

Mr. Cortez huffed. "I've heard the opposite."

Cortez the Killer had struck an uneasy peace with Bathory, one the cat often broke with tooth and claw. Lady Lucy told Squirrel that Cortez was a werewolf, and Bathory was an ancient vampire king who'd paid a withered crone to channel his essence into the body of a cat so he might live forever. And, of course, there is old enmity between vampires and werewolves, so why would the two of them have anything but disdain for one another?

"Bathory has already brought us luck," said Lady Lucy.

"How do you figure?" asked Mr. Cortez.

"Bathory shows himself and the clouds part. We are on a night hunt. Now the moon lights our way."

"The better to see you with, my dear."

"Do you intend to eat us, Mr. Cortez?"

"No, I don't believe I will."

"Splendid. Then let us proceed."

And we did, Mr. Cortez at the stern, paddling, Lady Lucy in the middle, whispering spells into the night with tears in her eyes. Drink and darkness made Lady Lucy melancholy, but it was more than that. Muted singing carried across the surface of the water; greenteeth songs were always sad. I ran my fingers through Bathory's fur, took comfort in the low rumble of his purring. Squirrel grew smaller against the black horizon, and if not for the moon and the candlelit windows on either side of the street, she'd have vanished entirely. We were a year removed from the hurricane, from the day our parents were taken, and in all that time Squirrel and I had never been apart.

We were a matched set, me and Squirrel.

I wasn't sure either of us could exist without the other.

The boat cut a path between two palm trees, fronds poking up above the surface of the water. Somewhere below was my mother's bakery, my father's auto repair shop, the weedy alleys where Squirrel and I chased one another on bicycles, and the convenience store where we bought fried burritos and orange sodas. Somewhere below was the low-slung pink bungalow where we'd lived until the water came in a rush and erased our lives. The four of us had made it onto the roof, but that wasn't high enough. Our parents sent Tina up the oak tree that leaned out over the house; she moved up it fast as a squirrel, earned the nickname I gave her. I followed, feeling the whipcrack of the wind against my cheeks. Then the water broke over the roofline of the house like a conquering army. Our parents were gone in a moment. We told everyone the greenteeth drew them down, like that was a better way to go than dying in the storm. Regardless, we never saw them again, though I was afraid one day we might.

Mr. Cortez navigated between buildings, their windows glowing with candlelight. Occasional faces peered out, likely certain we traveled to our doom. It was a couple of miles from the bookstore to what used to be the shoreline, and the water ahead rippled with fish or with greenteeth; I couldn't say which. Nothing broke the surface, but the air smelled like a beached whale left to die in the sunshine. Bathory clawed at the cold air, hissed at the horizon.

"Bathory insists you paddle faster," said Lady Lucy.

Mr. Cortez had already worked up a sweat, and I was certain we were traveling as fast as his strength could carry us.

"I won't take orders from a cat," he said.

"Bathory is more than a cat."

"We agree on that," he said. "He's something worse. I've seen that animal lap up a saucer of warm blood."

"You have not."

"Well, I saw him drink something."

"Call in the witchfinder."

Mr. Cortez smiled. "You know I bow to your whims, Lady, but the cat can go hang."

Bathory hissed again, but this time with more urgency, and he drew our attention to the water ahead.

A face broke the surface.

It was a greentooth woman with her chin barely above water, long hair trailing in the current. Green moss grew along her teeth, clogged her nostrils, and rimmed her eyes, like the stuff had taken root inside her and was working its way out. She was bloodless. Ashen. Her mouth opened wide in song, and the sound burrowed into my chest. Cut my nerve. The oar stopped, and Cortez the Killer had his pistol in hand. Would a bullet harm a greentooth? Lady Lucy often compared them to sirens, creatures who sang sailors down to their deaths, except the greenteeth were different. They wore the faces of people you knew. They weren't monsters. They were the dead come back to help us cross over. Mr. Cortez mumbled in Spanish, eyes wide and teary. And a name appeared on his lips, one he repeated over and over: *Marta, Marta, Marta.*

Cortez the Killer was transfixed. I thought of Miracle on her balcony, waiting to be drawn down while Lady Lucy watched. Mr. Cortez holstered his gun, turned the boat so that the greentooth woman floated right alongside.

Marta, Marta, Marta.

He put a trembling hand out over the water, nearly close enough to touch her, like he wanted to make sure she was real. I believe he'd have left us there, climbed out into the water and allowed himself to be taken down, if not for Lady Lucy.

She put her hands on his cheeks, cupped his face, and drew his eyes to hers. "Today is not the day to follow, sweet one. Your Marta will be there for you. When you're ready. You have reason to live yet."

Mr. Cortez closed his eyes, kept them closed tight until finally the greentooth woman sank below the waterline. The itchy feeling of her enchantment relented, and he pressed his face against Lady Lucy's neck and cried.

"Can you paddle us for a bit, Rowdy?" she asked.

"Yes, ma'am."

She handed me the oar, and I did my best to get us moving again in the right direction.

"It was my wife," said Mr. Cortez.

"I know," said Lady Lucy. "I met her a few times before the storm."

"Of course. I'd forgotten," said Cortez. "She loved to read. Nothing fancy, though. Trashy romances. Horror novels with blood and skulls on the cover."

"A woman after my own heart."

Mr. Cortez wiped his eyes with a shirtsleeve and straightened his hat so it fell at the correct, rakish angle. I'd overheard enough of their conversations to know Marta had been one of the first storm survivors to be drawn down by the greenteeth. Their grandkids had been visiting for the summer when the water came and carried both children away. That loss broke Marta, and when they came bobbing up at her balcony, singing a nursery song she'd taught them from her own childhood, she followed without a second thought.

"Rowdy, have a care," said Lady Lucy. "You're splashing about with that oar, and my cloak is getting wet."

The rain had started in earnest again, and I figured my splashing was the least of her worries, but I wasn't one to argue.

"Sorry, Lady."

"I don't want to die," said Mr. Cortez. "Not yet."

"Of course you don't," said Lady Lucy. "That's why I stopped you."

"But I *should* want to die, shouldn't I? They're all gone. And here I am, with you. I should have let her take me."

"You should do precisely what you wish. The dead have no say in our lives apart from what we give them."

Bathory climbed over Lady Lucy's lap and squeezed in beside Mr. Cortez. He scratched the scruff of Bathory's neck, in spite of himself.

Lady Lucy had a story about the greenteeth. It started with a hurricane so bad everybody remembered it a hundred fifty years later. Close to ten thousand dead, and the worst thing to happen to the island until last year, when the ocean swallowed it up for good. She believed Galveston was a place where the dead never left. They just *waited*. She called the greenteeth *embodiments of our collective despair*, which I took to mean they were there to make sure we never forgot we'd be with them one day, beneath the waves. The storm we survived changed the island's nature, thinned the barrier between life and afterlife. I wasn't sure if the Lady's take on the greenteeth was as fanciful as her other stories, but it was one we believed.

The greenteeth never took anyone by force. But they were there to help you die, whenever you were ready.

I paddled harder, hoping Squirrel wasn't ready.

I had no desire to leave this world yet, no matter the weight of my memories. But anxiety kept reminding me that tragedy burdens us all in different ways, and there was really no way of knowing how close Squirrel was to leaving all of this behind.

We reached what used to be the shoreline. The Hotel Galvez rose high above the water, several of its stories consumed forever by the sea. Debris crowded against the walls of the old hotel: shredded bits of wood that used to be a pier; the partial arc of a fallen Ferris wheel; street signs and broken concrete and coils of electrical line.

Squirrel was closer now. The water became choppy, and she had to slow her pace. Dozens of greenteeth swam in the deep waters, circling her boat, heads poking above the surface like shark fins. They sang their ghost songs. Cried with grief. The sounds they made carried over the surface of the water like slow winter fog, and froze my insides.

"They won't harm her," said Lady Lucy. "And they won't take her unless she wants to go."

"Okay, but what if she does?"

"Squirrel isn't ready to go yet," she said. "Oh, she's bored out of her skull like most of us. But there's still a whole lot left for her to accomplish in life. Might be she wants to leave and go to the mainland when she gets a bit older. I don't think I'm ever moving on from here. This is my home, flooded or not, and it always will be. But you can take her. Better than living out your life in a cave of books with an old lady who drinks too much. And besides, I know for certain Squirrel has no intention of letting the greenteeth draw her down today. Bathory assures me that is not her intention."

"Bathory is a cat."

"Bathory is my *familiar*." Our expedition had shaken her sober, but her dark mood still loomed like a storm cloud, ready to unleash a torrent if provoked.

"Lady Lucy, I appreciate you trying to make me feel better, but we need to get to Squirrel."

"Have I asked you to stop rowing?" she asked.

"No, ma'am."

"Well then, continue apace. And I will tell you a story. It begins with once upon a time."

"Of course it does."

Lady Lucy ignored my impatient tone and continued. "Once upon a time, there lived a sad drunk named Lucy who ruled an entire kingdom of books, but was forever thwarted in her pursuit of love. Not for lack of trying, you understand. She was no longer young, and no longer beautiful, if she'd ever been so in the first place, but she had a mind sharp as a samurai sword and certain skills with the dark arts, and so she whipped up a potion in an orange Tupperware mixing bowl and called out to the universe to send her someone to love. And whether by spell or by happenstance, a woman named Marjorie walked into her store the next day, with a midnight-black cat cradled in her arms. The cat's eyes flashed blood red and Marjorie's eyes were deep blue oceans, and Lady Lucy knew that a miracle had happened. Her dream now walked in waking hours. And they were happy, Lady Lucy and her miracle. Marjorie carried a heavy grief, having lost her only child some years before, but her grief and the Lady's sadness bookended a shared peace when they were together, and for a time they were content.

"But then the water came. A neglected world revolted. And what does the universe care about true love? Lucy and Marjorie moved their lives to higher ground, and even then, the Lady was certain her spell would hold. Their melancholy was enough to sustain them. They read passages from *The Tombs of Atuan* to one another. Sang mournful songs like "Going to California" and "Black Hole Sun." They crafted joy from nothing. But Marjorie's grief was so close to the surface. It was hard to resist. And eventually she couldn't.

"I've told you about Miracle going into the water, but sweet Bathory, with his old soul, helped me understand it was her choice. There was no love I could give greater than the one she'd lost. Who would I be if I stopped her? But less than a fortnight after Miracle left, Bathory spotted my little darlings at the window, with their empty bellies and their sinking boat. Scavengers barely holding on to life. He bid me invite you in, and here we are. A sort of family. All of this is to say, when you have loved someone so very near to death, you come to understand what it looks like. And I promise you, our darling Squirrel is nowhere close to giving up her ghost."

That may be as close as Lady Lucy ever came to telling her true story, though who can say. It didn't matter. Our stories were all we had left. Even if they weren't true, they were still ours.

"Thank you, Lady," I said.

"Thank Bathory," she said. "If not for his benevolence, you might still be scratching at my window, begging to be let in."

We drew within fifty yards of Squirrel's boat. Cortez the Killer took back the oar, and we soon bridged the distance. Greenteeth swarmed in the water, popped their heads up to look, then dived back down. There were dozens. Squirrel's tiny boat rocked in the wake of their passage, and she sat motionless. My worries grew teeth. As soon as Mr. Cortez had us alongside Squirrel's boat, I climbed into it, put my arms around her. But holding her did little to calm my distress. Squirrel's heart raced. She was hyperventilating. She felt insubstantial, ready to slip away from me again. A pair of greenteeth floated ahead of the boat, commanded Squirrel's attention, and no matter what Bathory might think, she was drawn to them. A man and a woman. Faces flooded with grief and voices full of static. One had eyes with my same shade of green, and another had long black curls that matched Squirrel's. And I understood. They looked so much like our parents; how could Squirrel not have followed them? Those faces seemed so familiar, like faded photograph versions of the people our parents had been, but when I looked closer, when I forced myself to see them as they were, and not as I wanted them to be, I knew for certain these were other souls.

Our parents were close, though. I knew that much.

They watched us every day through Lady Lucy's window. They pressed their ears against the glass in the deep night, listened to our cackling laughter and our arguments. They drifted just below the water's surface, in the land of the dead, but within easy reach. So, yeah, they were close. But the greenteeth floating in front of us were strangers. We'd see our parents again someday, but if I knew one thing for certain, it was they'd never want either of us to follow them down below until we'd had a chance to live our lives.

"It's not them, Tina."

She wouldn't stop shaking, wouldn't look away from the faces in the water. They offered a cold, wet death, and I knew how hard I would fight to keep her from leaving me.

"Tina, listen to me. It's Rowdy. It's Adam."

"I found them," she said. "Mom and Dad."

"That's not them. Look at me, please." I turned her to face me. I gave her a gentle shake, like I was trying to wake her up in time for school.

"Adam?"

"Yeah, it's me."

The greenteeth kept singing, but Squirrel rubbed her eyes and slowed her breathing. The effects of the song began to fade.

"I don't think it's them," she said.

"You're safe, Tina."

She shook her head. "God, I'm stupid."

"You're not stupid."

Squirrel started to cry. She hugged me. Held on tight, like she hadn't entirely escaped the greenteeth's pull.

"They swam by," she said, "and I could have waked you, but I didn't want you to die. And I guess I don't either, but I *needed* to see them. They just passed by so fast, and it was like they were leaving again, and I didn't know what to do. And now all of you, having to come out here. I'm so sorry."

"It's okay."

"Nothing is okay, Adam," she said. "I miss them."

"They'll be there, when you're ready. But you're not ready, right? You don't want to go to them?"

Squirrel looked back at the creatures in the water, and I held my breath, hoping the allure was not too much for her to resist. Hoping she felt life had more to offer her than death.

"No, not today," she said.

"I'm glad to hear it," I said. "Can we go home?"

"We don't have a home."

"Maybe not our old home, but we have someplace we're welcomed. Come on, okay? Lady Lucifer and her devil cat have missed you an awful lot."

"What did you call me?" asked Lady Lucy.

Squirrel held back a grin. I felt something loosen inside her, and she no longer seemed to be slipping away. "Thank you. All of you."

Cortez the Killer doffed his hat. "Always at your service, little Squirrel."

Lady Lucy had a tight grip on the gunwale of our boat, afraid perhaps we'd drift off the edge of the world and she'd have to follow. "We were given very little choice. Bathory was quite insistent. And as you well know, he is not to be trifled with."

Bathory hissed a storm and Lady Lucy whispered a few ancient spells, and eventually the two greenteeth vanished into the sea. All the others followed. Squirrel handed me her oar, and I paddled us toward our neighborhood. Cortez the Killer set a pace right behind us, and our travels home were untroubled by pirates or dead memories.

After that day, Mr. Cortez became a regular visitor to the book cave, and despite loud objections, Lady Lucy and Bathory both appreciated his company. Squirrel and I began to plan. We discussed places we might travel when we were old enough to fend for ourselves. I suggested someplace with snowcapped mountains, where rising tides would never trouble us, but Squirrel insisted on a city with an amusement park, and of course there was no reason to limit ourselves. We had a lifetime to explore. We settled in with our new family and made the book-stuffed apartment the best home we could. We'd sing all our sad songs, and Lady Lucy would recite epic poems. Cortez the Killer would tell us time and again about the pirate raid, but no two tellings were ever the same. Squirrel would dig through the shelves, finding books Lady Lucy had forgotten she owned, including a history of that long-ago hurricane that leveled the island, and how everyone came together then, to rebuild what was lost. Squirrel and I would drink cans of flat Dr. Pepper while Cortez the Killer sipped whiskey, and Lady Lucy grew maudlin from her wine. We'd stay up deep into the night, sharing memories of those who'd gone. Mom and Dad. Miracle and Marta. We told stories to keep them close.

Stories, maybe, to keep them away.

And some of those stories, though certainly not all of them, were true.

STORY NOTES

See That My Grave Is Kept Clean

The bone men came first. Just an image that invaded my mind and refused to leave. Caretakers for the graveyard, and who wouldn't wish for such attendants to our endless afterlives?

This whole collection is obsessed with death. With the mystery. And the protagonist in this story takes that obsession way too far. But it's hard not to, right? When you've lost someone you love so much. When maybe it's your fault.

Guilt and grief are inextricably bound.

So, I'm imagining those kindly bone men and listening to a lot of Phoebe Bridgers, and I realize that her song "Funeral" is the perfect vibe for what I want to write. I take that song into my bones. Let it make me miserable. The good kind of miserable, where you can stop feeling that way when the song ends.

Read enough of my work and you'll know every story has a song at its heart. A feeling that I'm trying to capture. Bridgers singing *Jesus Christ, I'm so blue all the time* was the perfect encapsulation of that feeling.

This is one of the grimmest stories I've written, but even so, there are threads of hope in it.

At least, I think there are.

＊

The Cure for Boyhood

Who wouldn't want to be a coyote? When I was a teenager, my friends and I were half feral already. Waiting for night to fall. Roaming the streets in packs.

The town I grew up in was small. A long way from anywhere. It's a place I love being *from*. But I can remember that restless version of myself who just wanted to run. The kid who was desperate to show everyone he was way too cool for that place, even though he knew in his heart he wasn't.

But readers take what they want from stories, and they have a habit of surprising the writer. A whole lot of folks read this as a different sort of allegory.

And when I read the story again, man . . . they're right.

This one is about being exactly who it is you want to be, no matter what other people might expect from you. Become that person. Transform. Don't let small minds set boundaries for you.

You only get one life.

*

Sounds Like Forever

Not the first time I've written about dead rock stars. Not likely the last. Jen in Sounds Like Forever is on the run from her life, and when that's happening to a person, there's no better place to hide than music. Particularly when music is your religion.

Here's a playlist to get you in the right headspace for this story. I had this dream about driving Jen's Fiero through a midnight thunderstorm, and when I woke, I was clutching a hand labeled Maxell cassette with these songs recorded on it.

So, gather your most dangerous friends. Make sure it's dark. Make sure it's raining. Close your eyes and listen. Maybe things are too much to handle right now. But music is there for you. Music makes everything better.

Veruca Salt—"Get Back"
Temple of the Dog—"Say Hello 2 Heaven"
Mother Love Bone—"Man of Golden Words"
Mazzy Star—"Flowers in December"
Nirvana—"Aneurysm"
PJ Harvey—"Down by the Water"
Soundgarden—"The Day I Tried to Live"
The Cure—"The Same Deep Water as You"
Jeff Buckley—"Lover, You Should've Come Over"
The Jesus and Mary Chain—"Never Saw It Coming"
Alice in Chains—"We Die Young"
Love and Rockets—"This Heaven"
Nine Inch Nails—"Something I Can Never Have"

This story is dedicated to Andrew Wood.
January 8, 1966—March 19, 1990

✳

Their Blood Smells of Love and Terror

Oh, *The Deadlands*. It's not just a place, it's a magazine. One of my favorites to emerge in recent years. Stories of death and the afterlife. Stories that interrogate that mystery. And since you're holding a collection about death and transformation, you need not wonder at the fondness I hold in my heart for that publication.

The Deadlands is responsible for this folk horror story. I desperately wanted to write something for them. So, I took my graveyard shovel from the bloody corner of the garage, and plunged it into the fallow earth. Over and over. Dug deep in that consecrated spot of land between *The Wicker Man* and "The Lottery," and struck bones.

I assembled those bones. Connected them together in various ways. Shaped the skeletons into a dozen different monsters. Mixed and matched them until I realized exactly what I'd disinterred from that mass grave and given new life.

Not monsters, but humans.

Thing is, it's hard to spot the difference.

*

A Red Promise in the Palm of Your Hand

Best way to read this story is by the light of a sputtering candle, in a rickety old cabin, a thousand miles from anywhere, with the wind rattling the walls and threatening to yank the house from its foundation.

If you can't manage that, you can read it in bed with the nightlight on, while a thunderstorm rages outside, but you're going to miss some of the loneliness.

Maybe you can get in the right mood if you think about broken promises. Things you used to believe with all your heart that don't ring true anymore. Are you going to follow those old beliefs to the death, or are you going to determine your own course? These are terrible questions to ask in the dark.

Eventually you'll hear the flutter of wings. You'll think maybe there are voices whispering words you don't want to hear. But that can't be. You're all alone.

Doesn't matter if you're in that creepy cabin or tucked in your warm bed. You're stuck in your head now, and there's nobody coming to help you.

But that doesn't mean nobody is coming.

Now you feel the loneliness, right? And the growing fear that all your choices have led you to this, and it's far too late to rethink any of them. Everything you're afraid of is right around the next corner.

You can grow wings and fly away. It's worth a shot, I guess.

But I don't think you'll get very far.

*

We Share Our Rage with the River

The Brazos River runs muddy. Not an ideal home for a mermaid, but better than living on land. Particularly the patch of land where this story takes place.

The men in this story like to own things. They will furiously defend all they've stolen from the victims of their crimes. They'll worship weapons. Build walls. Command obedience. It's all about personal freedom, yeah?

Except not for everyone. Some folks need to keep quiet. Some folks need to be told what's best for them. So, these men who own the land will bark and whine if you get out of line. But listen close and you'll hear the fear in their voices.

Fear of anybody different. Fear that somebody unworthy might get a small leg up in the world. Fear that the women in their lives might open their mouths, and reveal uncomfortable truths.

I'm pretty sure the mermaids are coming after them all.

And the mermaids are pissed.

*

Love Kills

Dying has to mess you up, right? Assuming you figure out a way to come back. Are you diminished a little more every time? And how long before you decide you've had enough?

Those of you who've been keeping score know that I'm pretty obsessed with Joe Strummer, the late lead singer of The Clash. I've written a couple of stories about the mythology surrounding him. This isn't one of those, necessarily, but it was inspired by one of his songs.

"Love Kills" is a solo effort from Joe, from the soundtrack to the film *Sid and Nancy*. A song about Sid Vicious. A song about selfish and toxic love. That's where my story comes in. There are no punk icons here, but the message of the song was a perfect fit. And so was the title.

A line from "Love Kills" ran on repeat in my brain while I wrote this: *but if my hands are the color of blood, then baby I can tell you, sure I can tell you, love kills.*

Love is pretty dangerous stuff in this story.

Thanks for the inspiration, Joe.

*

Constellation Burn

West Texas is vast. If you've never traveled out that way, I'm not sure you can appreciate the way it haunts you. The way it unfolds like a story with no end, one that never changes no matter how many times it's told.

Flat and wild and forever lonely.

West Texas is also an easy place to get lost. Especially if that's your goal. Speed limits are just a suggestion out there, and the highways unspool in endless straight lines. Drive deep into the heart of that place and the surreality of existence begins to consume you.

The people you meet are wild at heart and mad from the heat. They're escaping from old lives and chasing new ones. Deep West Texas calls to prophets and cultists and madmen. Wilderness enthusiast, faith healers, and bunker building survivalists.

The grim beauty of the place is infectious.

So is its paranoid nature.

Wander long enough and you might feel like you've fallen into a David Lynch movie. Wild eyes watching your every move. Scenery burned gold and brown by the relentless sun. Find yourself a lawn chair and a cold beer, cop a seat and let the heat melt away the last bit of your sanity. Nothing much matters out here.

Do you want to go home, or have you found a new one?

When night falls, the stars will come alive in those black skies. Look up and you'll find the Seven Sisters.

They may not lead you back out again, but they'll lead you somewhere. Whether you want to follow or not is up to you.

✱

The Green Realm

I have San Antonio writer Clayton Hackett to thank for this one. A while back he posted on social media about the Richard Butner collection, *The Adventurists*, describing it as "Gen X slipstream nostalgia." Yeah, that hooked me. That's a vibe I can get behind.

Clayton was right. The Butner collection was fantastic. Reading it put me in the mood to write something that's hard to put your arms around. Something that squirms out of your grip.

The characters in this story are lost, whether they know it or not. The selves they knew are fading away, replaced by the people they're going to become. People they might not like. Trees all around and it's tough to see what's ahead. Something is lurking. But what are you going to do? It's impossible to go backward, so you've got to keep moving.

I like that this is a bigfoot story that doesn't necessarily have a bigfoot in it. That's for the reader to decide, I guess. But there's *something* in those woods.

✱

Till the Greenteeth Draw us Down

We all lose people, but they never leave us. They remain there in our memories, so close we feel like we can reach out and touch them, and yet frustratingly distant. We think about joining them some day, and though we're in no rush to do so, the idea of them waiting there for us can be a comfort.

This story started with that not entirely unpleasant notion, and it mingled with legends about sea people, and sirens, and English folk tales about Jenny Greenteeth, a hag who lives in rivers and pulls people down to their deaths. My greenteeth are less insistent than Jenny, but no less eager for us to join them below the water.

The island city of Galveston has survived more than its share of overpowering hurricanes. The Great Storm of 1900 killed thousands of people, and I explored that event in my novel, *The Legend of Charlie Fish*. The hurricane that flooded the city in this story was just as bad, but unlike all the other storms, this one never left.

The dead remain. They're close, always watching.

It may not be time to join them yet. But when that time comes, they'll draw you down. They'll welcome you home.

All you have to do is close your eyes.

ACKNOWLEDGMENTS

A whole lot of people deserve thanks for helping shape these stories, this collection, and my years as a writer. I'm certain to leave out some-one deserving of thanks, so if that's you, I'm sorry. You're awesome!

Thanks to the super team at Underland Press for bringing this book to life: Mark Teppo, John Klima, and Darin Bradley. And to my agent, Kris O'Higgins, for helping to herd my career in the right directions. You all rock!

Thanks to the editors who first published these stories in their mag-azines and anthologies: Laura Blackwell, Scott Campbell, Kat Day, Shawn Garrett, Alex Hofelich, William Jensen, Michael Kelly, Erik Secker, and E. Catherine Tobler.

Thanks to my friends in the writing community who were subjected to early versions of these stories, and those who've been crazy enough to offer critical eyes and moral support for the longer stuff too: Douglas Gwilym, Clayton Hackett, Samantha Henderson, C.S. Humble, Derek Austin Johnson, Rick Klaw, Ryan Leslie, Jaime Lee Moyer, Frank Oreto, and Mikal Trimm.

And thanks to my wife, Kristin. Always my biggest supporter, and my travel companion down every weird road I've ever followed. Love you bunches.

ABOUT THE AUTHOR

Josh Rountree has published over 60 stories in a wide variety of magazines and anthologies, including *Beneath Ceaseless Skies, Realms of Fantasy, Bourbon Penn, Polyphony 6, Pseudo-Pod, PodCastle, Daily Science Fiction*, and *A Punk Rock Future*. A handful of them have received honorable mention in *The Year's Best Fantasy & Horror* and *The Year's Best Science Fiction*.

Wheatland Press published a collection of his rock and roll themed fantasy fiction, *Can't Buy Me Faded Love*, in 2008. His second collection, *Fantastic Americana: Stories*, was published by Fairwood Press. *Death Aesthetic* is his third collection.

Josh lives somewhere in the untamed wilds of Texas with his wife and children.

PUBLICATION HISTORY

"See That My Grave Is Kept Clean" originally appeared in *Pseudo-Pod*, 2023.

"The Cure for Boyhood" originally appeared in *Bourbon Penn*, 2021.

"Sounds Like Forever" originally appeared in *Bourbon Penn*, 2022.

"Their Blood Smells of Love and Terror" originally appeared in *The Deadlands*, 2022.

"A Red Promise in the Palm of Your Hand" originally appeared in *Weird Horror*, 2021.

"We Share Our Rage with the River" originally appeared in *Road Kill: Texas Horror by Texas Writers Volume 7*, 2022.

"Love Kills" originally appeared in *The Arcanist*, 2021.

"Constellation Burn" originally appeared in *Bourbon Penn*, 2023.

"The Green Realm" is previously unpublished.

"Till the Greenteeth Draw Us Down" originally appeared in *The Deadlands*, 2023.

Printed in the USA
CPSIA information can be obtained
at www.ICGtesting.com
LVHW041346200824
788529LV00004B/121